DARK VENDETTA

Simon Larren Thrillers
Book Two

Robert Charles

SAPERE
BOOKS

DARK VENDETTA

Published by Sapere Books.

20 Windermere Drive, Leeds, England, LS17 7UZ,
United Kingdom

saperebooks.com

ISBN: 978-1-80055-683-6

CHAPTER 1: THE SINKING OF THE *VIGILANT*

The explosion came as a complete shock; a heart-stopping, brain-tearing impact that crippled ship and men alike. At one moment *Vigilant* was cruising slowly at periscope depth, the next she was slammed sideways with savage, stunning force. She reared like a threshing whale, lifting half out of the water in one wild, upward lunge. The sea that a moment ago had been calm and placid boiled and surged around her steel-plated casing, beating at her in disturbed fury until she sank back into a maelstrom of foam.

High above, the Chinese pilot of the Russian-built Mig fighter watched with mixed feelings as he brought his plane wheeling round in a tight circle through the sky. He knew that his missile had not scored a direct hit for the submarine had not blown up, but her violent reaction showed that he had achieved a very near miss. The rocket he had fired had exploded on hitting the surface of the water just beside her.

He hesitated for a few seconds and then began calling the surface ships below.

In the control room of *Vigilant* there was chaos. Men had been hurled about like rag dolls. Her Captain, Lieutenant-Commander Rogerson, sprawled unconscious on the steel deck, blood staining his dark hair just above the left ear. Stanton, the Navigation Officer was on his knees, gasping and retching. There wasn't one man on his feet. Every light had smashed with the impact and the submarine was totally blacked out.

Vigilant writhed in a whirlpool of her own making and then her bows dipped and her deck canted at an angle; out of control she began sliding down towards the seabed.

In the officers' wardroom First-Lieutenant Waverly, the sub's Number One, picked himself up from the deck where he had been thrown against the bulkhead. He swayed groggily and then began to grope around the wardroom until he found an emergency torch. He could hear one of the stewards moaning as he flashed the torch on, but he didn't stop to look for the man. His ears were ringing and he was still dazed, but one thing was clear; he had to get to the control room. *Vigilant*, Britain's latest and finest nuclear submarine, was plunging straight for the bottom.

He stumbled out of the wardroom and found himself running downhill as the deck tilted steeply forwards. He heard another man behind him as he reached the control room and together they stumbled inside.

Waverly flashed his torch around the shambles of groaning men. Only Stanton was on his feet, looking grey and shocked in the torchlight. The rating who had followed Waverly blurted out hoarsely, "the Old Man," and pushed past to reach the still figure of Rogerson.

Waverly said harshly. "Damn the Old Man, the ship's sinking. Man the hydroplanes."

The rating looked up slowly, and then Naval discipline took over and he jumped to obey, clamping both hands on the large wheel that controlled the stern hydroplanes. Stanton stepped over the limp figure of a coxswain and manned the fore planes. Waverly took the helm and rapped out a string of orders.

Stanton spun his wheel, his eyes on the large depth gauges. He said savagely. "She won't answer. She won't answer the controls."

Tense seconds passed and then Waverly said tightly:

"She's coming."

Slowly *Vigilant* answered the sweating hands at the controls. Her bows began to lift as she stopped her downward plunge to the ocean floor, gradually she levelled out and began to nose forward through the depths.

The ratings on the floor were beginning to sort themselves out. Only Rogerson was still unmoving. The asdic rating pulled himself back into his seat and stared at his equipment. With an effort he adjusted his earphones. He said sharply:

"There's a surface vessel coming straight for us, sir. It sounds like a destroyer."

Waverly felt a sickening, tightening sensation in his stomach and knew that his situation was desperate. There had been a lot of doubts about sending *Vigilant* into Chinese territorial waters to investigate the strange new shore installations in Choohow Bay, and now it seemed that the more cautious officers back at headquarters had been right.

Somehow *Vigilant* had been detected, and the Chinese were taking their heaven-sent opportunity to move in for the kill before she could regain international waters and the safe depths of the open sea.

Grimly Waverly took control, ordering avoiding action.

The ratings who had been on duty at the hydroplane controls were now recovered enough to resume their posts, and Stanton was able to attend to the Commander who was still lying on the deck. At the same moment Lieutenant Harlow, the ship's Third Officer, arrived with Sub-Lieutenant Bennet on his heels.

Waverly felt a little better on having his fellow officers to support him and sent Bennet to check the rest of the ship and report the damage. Two ratings were detailed to carry the unconscious Rogerson to his stateroom.

A few seconds later the Chinese destroyer passed overhead and the first rain of depth charges began to explode around them. The wavering lights of the emergency torches jerked wildly as the ship shuddered and groaned. Waverly snapped more orders and *Vigilant* responded clumsily to her controls as she twisted through the depths to avoid the attack. Waverly knew that one or more of the hydroplane fins must have been damaged by that first crippling explosion.

High above, the Mig pilot watched the destroyer circling the spot where the submarine had vanished, a sleek grey killer carving twin walls of white foam from the blue seas at the bows. The pilot watched for a moment and then obeyed the curt voice in his earphones that was ordering him to return to base. The submarine was too deep for him to do any good now and he knew that his Commanding Officer was not going to be pleased at his failure to destroy the spy-ship completely.

Nervous tension was stirring at his stomach as his fighter disappeared over the low hills of the China coastline.

Down below the destroyer was coming back for its second attacking run.

In the pitch darkness that filled *Vigilant* Sub-Lieutenant Bennet was making his way slowly aft when the second series of depth charges hurled him off his feet. *Vigilant* bucked wildly and trembled from stem to stern. More shocks vibrated around her and then she steadied again.

Bennet groped for his torch and carried on. His hand was slippery around the torch as he crossed a catwalk that led past the reactor and he paused above the engine room. His whole body went cold as he heard the chilling sound of water pouring through ruptured plates. More men with torches were moving below him and in the ghastly half light he saw a miniature flood bursting through the far bulkhead.

Heath, the Engineering Officer, staggered towards him. He was dripping wet and smeared with oil, his face was tight and pale as he stared up the ladder to where the Sub-Lieutenant was standing.

"What the hell's happening?"

Bennet tried to sound calm. "I'm not really sure, Chief. We've obviously been spotted and at the moment there's a destroyer hunting us. What's the situation here?"

"Bloody rough. Half my men are unconscious and the other half hardly know what they're doing."

"Can you keep the engines going?"

"Of course I can, it's my job isn't it." Heath sounded offended.

"What about that leak?"

"It's not too serious — looks worse than it is." Heath turned away, back towards the splashing, cursing men under his command. "I'll send up a report as soon as I can," he promised.

Bennet moved on, probing the inky blackness with his torch, blundering into frightened men from the off-duty watches and desperately trying to assess the real extent of the damage. It seemed that *Vigilant*'s plates had ruptured in several places and the sound of in-rushing seawater sounded above the shouts and curses of the crew.

Back in the control room Waverly was issuing order after order in an attempt to get clear of the pursuing destroyer, but still another series of depth charges tumbled through the seas around them. *Vigilant* was becoming gradually less responsive to the controls, despite everything the ratings at the hydroplanes could do.

Another near miss made *Vigilant* vibrate violently and then one of the hydroplane ratings finally had to report.

"The ship refuses to answer, sir. She's running wild."

Waverly turned to face the Navigation Officer.

"What course are we on?"

Stanton had the answer ready. "We're running approximately parallel to the coastline."

Waverly hesitated for half a second and then rapped:

"Let her run. Full ahead."

The order passed down the intercom to the engine room. Swiftly the revs built up, and the great propellers churned through the silent depths, sending *Vigilant* surging at full speed through the undersea world.

Waverly knew that he was very close to the bottom, and despite the most up-to-date echo-sounding equipment to measure the depth beneath him he was running a serious risk of crashing his ship into any ridge or sandbank on the ocean floor. But it was a risk that had to be taken. Speed was now *Vigilant*'s only chance of escape. Her nuclear-powered engine could give over twenty-five knots even under water, and the destroyer on the surface could not know that she was pursuing an atomic submarine; with luck the sheer, unexpected speed would take them clear.

A few seconds passed and silence reigned. No one spoke. Waverly's face was tight and strained in the sallow glow of the torches, Stanton and Harlow were sweating.

Then the asdic rating said grimly. "The destroyer's changed course, sir. She's coming after us."

"Steer ninety degrees port," rapped Waverly. "Try and turn her to the open sea."

Tense seconds crawled past. The ratings at the hydroplanes spun the control wheels grimly. One of them said tightly:

"The ship isn't answering, sir. She's still out of control."

"Keep trying. Maintain full speed."

They were the only orders Waverly could give. It was obvious now that the hydroplane fins were badly damaged; *Vigilant* could only race at full speed and parallel the Chinese coastline with no way of regaining the safe waters beyond the twelve miles that the Chinese claimed as their territorial limits. Her officers could only pray.

Somewhere out to sea the conventional submarine *Relentless* was standing by, but even if he could contact her Waverly knew that there was nothing she could do. *Vigilant* was entirely on her own, and *Relentless* might just as well be back in port.

Above them the destroyer let loose another barrage of depth charges and *Vigilant* squirmed again as the shock waves sent her reeling. The submarine jerked and rushed off on a slightly altered course that was bringing her ever closer to the Chinese shore. Fortunately the coastline was fairly level, with no jutting headlands that would have spelled the end for the runaway submarine. Even so the officers in the control room were sweating hard as they watched the depth gauges.

Then the destroyer was again lost and the asdic rating reported that the contact was fading.

Waverly began to breathe normally again.

He maintained full speed until he was sure he had given the destroyer the slip and then ordered the speed cut by half.

Bruised and battered *Vigilant* cruised through the depths, still on her runaway course.

Harlow and Stanton moved closer to Waverly and the three officers' held a hurried conference.

Their plight was serious. *Vigilant*'s steering gear was almost useless and the submarine was still practically out of control. And even though they had temporarily shaken off their pursuers they were still in enemy waters.

While they conferred Bennet returned with a fairly comprehensive report. *Vigilant*'s hull had sprung three more leaks apart from the one in the engine room, one was in the crew's quarters and two were in the forward torpedo room. The Petty Officers had regained some element of order and all the emergency torches were now in use. The number of men still suffering from shock or concussion from that first terrible explosion totalled almost a third of the crew, including the Commander who was still unconscious.

Waverly listened to Bennet's report and then turned to Heath, the Engineering Officer, who had just appeared, still dripping with oil and seawater.

Heath's report was shorter, but by far the most alarming. The engine room was under two foot of water and the pumps were hardly keeping it under control. There was also trouble with the generator and Heath feared an explosion.

Waverly hesitated for a long time before saying. "There's nothing we can do about the generator except trust to you, Chief, and hope. As for the steering problem it's obvious that we're not going to make any headway while we're submerged. We're nearly fifty miles south of the point where we were attacked so I'm going to chance surfacing as soon as it's dark. That's if we can surface. With luck we'll be able to manoeuvre up top, or at least repair the damage to the steering gear. Until then we'll lay on the bottom."

Harlow drew a deep breath. "What happens if the Chinese Navy is still waiting for us?"

Waverly shrugged. "We come back to the bottom — one way or another."

A few hours later Waverly decided that it must now be as dark on the surface as he could hope for and quietly he gave the order to raise *Vigilant* to periscope depth.

The submarine handled clumsily, stirring sluggishly through the sea. She was like some expiring sea-monster on the brink of death and it was with great difficulty that she was coaxed towards the surface. There were long moments when Waverly believed that she would never make it but at last she reached the required depth.

Waverly ordered the periscope up and rose up with it, the eyepiece clamped hard against his brows. The periscope broke the low waves on the surface and Waverly stopped its ascent with a wave of his hand to the rating at the control lever. Slowly he took a look round.

There was nothing in sight but the sea, dark, cold and restless, glinting slightly in the starlight. Slowly Waverly revolved the periscope, pausing as he found himself staring at the shoreline of China, a black, rising land mass that was barely three miles away. He realised that he was a lot closer than he had supposed and his lips tightened grimly.

He continued the slow sweep of the periscope but there was nothing else to be seen. *Vigilant* had the sea to herself.

Waverly made another sweep with the periscope, making doubly sure. It was quite possible that the Chinese had called off the hunt, believing that *Vigilant* had either escaped to deeper waters or was lying on the bottom some fifty miles back along the coast where she had been depth-charged. But it was also possible that although there were no ships in the vicinity to alarm him there might be aircraft waiting above the clouds, searching for the first signs as the submarine broke surface, the starlight glinting on the rocket warheads slung under their wings.

At last Waverly turned to his fellow officers.

He said quietly. "Maybe they're waiting for us. Maybe not. The only way to find out is to surface." He licked his lips and finished: "*Relentless* should be somewhere in the area, waiting for us to rejoin her. Before we make the attempt we'll send her a coded signal — that way they'll know what's happened if we don't make it."

He turned to the chart table and began to make out the signal to *Relentless*.

Leading Telegraphist James Andrews made the signal to *Relentless* three minutes later, making quick contact despite the fact that *Vigilant* was still submerged with only a few feet of her radio antenna protruding above the surface.

Andrews had almost finished the signal when a terrific explosion in the engine room shattered *Vigilant* from stem to stern. Her hull split wide open and the ship heeled over in agony as the sea burst in. The majority of her crew died instantly as she plunged back towards the bottom.

The gallant *Vigilant* had made her last signal.

CHAPTER 2: CONFERENCE

It was a magnificent morning. The tall, white skyscrapers of Hong Kong were painful to look at as they reflected the glare of the rising sun. The bright blue waters of the straits between the twin cities of Victoria and Kowloon were a dazzling playground for the busy ferries and the slower junks and sampans. The traffic was roaring down the main artery of Queen Street and the narrow side streets and alleyways were bustling with life and colour. It was soon after dawn and the restless colony of Hong Kong was impatient to begin the new day.

In the long conference room below the overshadowing mass of Victoria Peak there was no such bustle, no noise and no impatience. The amount of gold braid visible around the highly-polished surface of the long table was impressive to say the least. At the head of the table sat a grim-faced Admiral, a Vice-Admiral flanked him on each side; the rest of the group consisted of one Rear-Admiral, one Commodore, two Naval Commanders and one Lieutenant-Commander. Their faces were unsmiling as they faced the Admiral in command and waited. Most of them had no idea of why they had been called, but the Admiral's face showed that it was no reason for rejoicing.

The Admiral rose slowly to his feet and cleared his throat.

"Gentlemen," he began, "I think most of you were sitting at this very table some forty-eight hours ago when we discussed the proposition to send H.M.S. *Vigilant* to investigate the ominous amount of activity at Choohow Bay on the north coast of China. As you know the Communists are constructing some kind of shore installations there which we suspect to be of a military nature. And as it would be impossible for an aircraft to get near the area without being detected we decided to send *Vigilant* into Chinese waters in the hope that her Commander could learn something through her periscope. I regret to inform you, Gentlemen, that *Vigilant* was detected and attacked by the Chinese. She is missing and feared lost with all hands."

There was a tense silence. Expressions of shock and disbelief were registered on every face. The seven men seated around the conference table seemed frozen into immobility. No one moved or spoke. Then the pencil in the agitated hands of the Rear-Admiral snapped clean in two with a brittle crack.

The sound killed the silence and a grey-bearded Vice-Admiral asked slowly. "How did it happen?"

The Admiral drew a deep breath, and then explained all that he knew of *Vigilant*'s fate from her last signal which had been passed back to him by the submarine *Relentless*.

When he had finished the Vice-Admiral on his left said slowly: "I take it that there'll be an enquiry?"

His grey-bearded colleague said grimly. "There's sure to be. *Vigilant* was Britain's latest and most expensive nuclear submarine; she represents a hell of a lot of the tax-payer's money, and you can't hush up a loss like that." He stopped for a moment and then added. "There'll be trouble from the press too; once they discover that we've been using *Vigilant* to snoop around the Chinese coast it will make the stink that the Americans caused with their U2 spy-plane smell like a rosebud in a sewer bed."

The full Admiral nodded. "That's true, and I've no doubt that myself and one or two others who backed me up will feel the sharp edge of the axe. But that is not our immediate problem, gentlemen. It's too late to reconsider old decisions. *Vigilant*'s telegraphist was cut off in the middle of a word when he made her last signal, so we know that whatever happened to the submarine it happened very suddenly and very fatally. From that we can only assume that *Vigilant* is lying on the seabed at approximately the same position from which she made that signal. That fact is going to provide us with a far greater problem than the eventual fate of our private careers."

He paused again and leaned forwards slightly with both hands pressed down on the table. His forehead was deeply lined and in the shaded light of the conference room he looked suddenly and incredibly old.

He continued. "I have spent the last few hours studying the charts appropriate to that section of the Chinese coastline, and it appears that *Vigilant* is lying less than three miles off the coast and in not more than 240 feet of water. The problem of salvaging her will not prove a difficult one and the Communists will most certainly make the attempt once they locate her. *Vigilant* was carrying all the most up-to-date developments in underwater navigation, her design is still listed as top secret, and she is also equipped to fire Polaris missiles; she will provide invaluable information for the reds if they can bring her back to the surface. Somehow, gentlemen, we must ensure that *Vigilant* is totally destroyed. She must not be salvaged."

For a brief moment they digested his words and then the grey-bearded Vice-Admiral said grimly, "I believe *Relentless* is carrying a full armament of torpedoes; couldn't she creep along the bottom and fire the lot into *Vigilant*? The reds wouldn't learn much from the wreckage that would be left."

The Commodore jerked his head up sharply, speaking for the first time. "We can't do that! If *Vigilant* is down on the bottom then there may be men alive inside her. It would be murder!"

The grey beard bristled. "I obviously didn't mean that such action should be taken straight away. Enough time must elapse for us to be absolutely sure that *Vigilant*'s crew are dead and not still trying to escape."

The Rear-Admiral spoke, also for the first time. "By that time it will be too late. Once the Chinese locate *Vigilant* they will most certainly station a surface vessel over her until such time as they can start salvage operations. It will be impossible for us to take any action then."

The Commodore's hands clenched but he held himself in check. The angry silence was broken by the sound of a door opening.

The Admiral's personal secretary came inside. She was a tall, efficient-looking woman, and the set of nervous determination on her face indicated that she knew exactly what sort of reception to expect.

The Admiral glared at her angrily and his voice barked out like the roar of a gun.

"I thought I gave orders that I was not to be disturbed — not in any circumstances."

The woman winced but came resolutely forward. She held out a slip of white paper.

"A signal from *Relentless*, sir."

The Admiral hesitated. "My apologies. Thank you."

The secretary risked a half smile and then made a swift exit.

The Admiral read the signal and then glanced around the table. He said quietly, "*Relentless* reports increasing activity in the area, gentlemen. At least six destroyers are now patrolling the twelve mile limit, and are apparently trying to locate *Vigilant. Relentless* has retreated from the area."

The grey-bearded Vice-Admiral grimaced. "Then we definitely can't risk sending another submarine into Chinese waters."

"It seems that the destruction of the submarine is of more importance than the lives of her crew," returned the Commodore bitterly.

The full Admiral said sharply, "That is not so, Commodore — and you should know it. We are simply trying to face this problem rationally. *Vigilant* went down so fast that there can be very little possibility of any of her crew remaining alive. But even so no action of any kind will be taken until even the remotest possibility has vanished."

The second Vice-Admiral added, "We can only pray that any men who survived will be able to make their own escape from inside. And meanwhile we must find some way of destroying the submarine after they have had their chance, but before the Chinese can commence salvage operations."

There were slow nods of assent, and even the Commodore was forced to agree.

The full Admiral looked slightly relieved at these first signs of unity, and when he spoke again his voice was fully authoritative.

"Gentlemen, this situation has developed exactly as I expected, but fortunately Naval Intelligence has come up with at least one idea which I think deserves some consideration." He looked towards the blunt-jawed Naval Commander who had so far remained silent at the end of the table. "Commander Maclean, perhaps you will outline the plan you suggested to me before this conference began."

Maclean exchanged a momentary glance with Lieutenant-Commander Alan Kendall, his second in command, and then rose to his feet. A stray shaft of sunlight caught the silvery gleam of his temples and flickered over the hard set of his face.

He said flatly, "As you all know it was my suggestion that *Vigilant* should undertake her last mission, so naturally I've been keeping in close contact with the Admiral in regard to her movements. While we were waiting for you all to arrive we discussed the question of destroying *Vigilant*. We anticipated heavy surface patrols by the Chinese, for they will obviously prepare for any attempt on our part to ensure that *Vigilant* does not get salvaged. That means that to send in another submarine, or any kind of Naval vessel, would only mean more trouble. The use of aircraft is also out of the question, for *Vigilant* is too deep to be reached by bombing even if we dared risk such violation of Chinese air and sea space. That only leaves one other front for attack — the land.

"I propose, gentlemen, that we land a picked strike party of underwater saboteurs on the Chinese mainland. They can be landed well south of the patrolling destroyers from a fishing junk: That stretch of coastline is pretty barren and thinly populated, and providing the strike party keeps to the hills and moves only at night they should stand a good chance of circling north to the spot where *Vigilant* is assumed to be sunk. It should take them five or six days to get into position, and I think that if no survivors have been reported from *Vigilant* by that time then we must acknowledge the fact that they will all be dead. The strike party will then have to swim out and place a series of high-powered explosives around *Vigilant*'s hull, positioning them so that they totally wreck the equipment most likely to be of help to the Chinese. Afterwards they must retreat the way they have come. There is no other way of ensuring that *Vigilant*'s secrets do not fall into Communist hands."

Maclean finished his speech and waited for the storm.

Almost a thousand miles away in one of the large new buildings at Choohow Bay a similar conference was taking place. Another group of high-ranking officers were seated around an almost identical table, their faces fixed with solemn stares on the arrogant features of the Admiral addressing them. On the wall behind the Admiral's back hung a large flag bearing the emblem of Communist China. The Admiral was speaking in Chinese and his voice was thick and harsh.

"As you know, Comrades, yesterday afternoon an unidentified submarine was detected while spying in Chinese waters and was attacked by a fighter of our glorious air force. One of our destroyers continued the attack but the submarine escaped. At first it was thought that the enemy had fled into the open sea, but now we have reason to believe that this was not so. Last night a radio signal was intercepted from that submarine which informed us that she is still in Chinese territorial waters. She did not finish her signal so it seems most likely that she finally sank due to the terrible punishment inflicted on her by our glorious navy."

He reached for a glass of water by his right hand and swallowed half of it in one greedy movement of his throat. Replacing the glass he continued. "Unfortunately we missed the first part of that signal, so we do not know exactly where this submarine is located. What we do know is that she is a nuclear submarine and probably British. The very speed with which she escaped from our destroyer proves that she must have been atomic powered; and the fact that every top naval officer in Hong Kong was seen rushing into British Naval Headquarters in Victoria this morning seems to leave little doubt as to her nationality."

He stopped and gulped again at the glass of water.

He smacked his lips and went on. "That submarine will make an interesting prize, Comrades, and we are going to salvage her. At the moment we have destroyers patrolling the whole of this stretch of coastline to guard against any more intruders, and we have salvage vessels standing by to go into operation as soon as the submarine is located."

An aide came swiftly forward and re-filled the water glass as the Admiral's hand reached out for it. The Admiral swallowed deeply and then faced his audience again.

"There is just one more point. Our highly-respected Comrades of the Soviet Union are also interested in the salvaging of this submarine. And just in case it should prove difficult to locate they have sent two of their most highly-trained agents to approach the problem from a different angle."

The Admiral extended one hand towards the far end of the room and said grandly. "I introduce to you, Comrades Dressler and Reutall."

All eyes turned towards the two men who were standing with their backs to the wall. Dressler was a tall, bony creature wearing a neatly cut grey suit, his eyes were hidden behind thick horn-rimmed glasses and he held a silver-topped cane loosely in his right hand. Reutall was shorter and chubbier. He wore a suit of charcoal black and his hands and wrists were covered with long, tight-fitting black leather gloves. Both men smiled and nodded towards the circle of officers around the conference table.

The Admiral slopped more water into his throat and then said, "Comrades Dressler and Reutall are going to Hong Kong. Their job will be to try and find out the exact position of this spy-submarine from the British. I am told that in their line of work they are considered experts."

CHAPTER 3: STRIKE PARTY

It was late afternoon and the sun still blazed down from a perfect sky that was a patchwork quilt of downy white and brilliant blue. The ferries still buzzed across the turquoise waters of the straits, a few British and American warships lay at anchor in the harbour, grey and menacing in the harsh sunlight, and graceful junks with great square, coloured sails drifted lethargically by. The life of Hong Kong throbbed and pulsed through its garish streets and squalid alleys. Across the bay the hills behind Kowloon were a hazy purple in the distance.

Commander Charles Maclean was unaware of it all as he sat before the large desk in his bright, air-conditioned office. He was hatless and in his shirtsleeves and there was a trickle of sweat making its way slowly down the side of his face. The touch of silver at his temples made him look several years older than he really was, and at the moment his face was hard and strained.

The clash of wills over his proposed solution to the problem of *Vigilant* had been much tougher than he had expected, and some of the men he had had to convince had been openly hostile. He had been prepared for that to a certain extent, for the fact that the Intelligence department had requested that *Vigilant* investigate Choohow Bay could not help coming under criticism. But the weight and bitterness behind the attack had surprised and startled him, and his new proposition had met some stiff opposition.

Finally the support of the Admiral had helped him to push the plan through, for it was clear that there was no other way of preventing the submarine from falling into Chinese hands. He had eventually escaped from the conference room feeling mentally battered, but at least he had won his point. The strike party was to be formed and landed on the mainland with all possible speed, and it was left to the Intelligence department to work out the final details.

He had worked at the problem all day; studying charts of the coastline and selecting the right spot to land his men, arranging for the Captain of a broken-down fishing junk to smuggle them into Chinese waters, and contacting experts on everything from underwater sabotage to emergency battle rations. He had only to close his eyes and he could see the complete chart of the Chinese coast printed indelibly on the inside of his eyelids, and his brain was throbbing from the effort of trying to control the mass of facts and figures he had gathered.

He stared wearily at the mass of papers that littered his desk and realised that now there was only one major task left: he had to explain to the man whom he hoped would put his head not only in the lion's mouth but halfway down its gullet.

There was a sudden knock on his office door and then Alan Kendall came in. The Lieutenant-Commander was a young man for his rank, but the set of his lips and jawline showed that he was fully aware of its responsibilities.

He said briefly, "I've located Captain Mason, sir. He was sunbathing on the beach at Repulse Bay."

Maclean said quietly, "How did he react?"

Kendall grinned. "Quite amiably. There was a half-naked blonde with him, but he seemed to think that the hero-worship in her eyes was sufficient compensation for leaving her company. He quite enjoyed having a Lieutenant-Commander in full uniform come to fetch him."

"Where is he now?"

"Waiting outside, sir. I brought him back with me."

Maclean sighed. "Show him in will you, we may as well get it over with."

Kendall nodded and went out of the room. He returned a few seconds later with a tall, bronzed man wearing casual fawn trousers and a bright red shirt. The shirt was short-sleeved and tucked elegantly in the throat was a light cravat of white silk.

Maclean stared and Kendall said quickly. "I brought Captain Mason straight up from the beach, sir. As the matter was urgent I didn't waste time in getting him into uniform."

Maclean hesitated, and for a moment he wondered whether he was entrusting this mission to the right man. Then he recalled Mason's record and his doubts were dispelled. Paul Mason had the nonchalant manner of a sporting wastrel, and the cravat, which he habitually wore as a mark of his individuality, added a touch of dandified elegance that was highly deceptive. It was only after the second look that you noted the hard, muscular arms and the brisk movements of a man at the peak of physical fitness, and the unflinching clarity in his blue gaze indicated an easy self-confidence.

Paul Mason was a Captain in the Royal Marines, and despite the flamboyant touch to his nature he was a good officer. He was also an excellent swimmer and had been trained in the delicate art of underwater sabotage. He had the look of a man who knew exactly where he was going in life, the shortest route of getting there, and how to deal with any kind of trouble that might come up along the way.

Maclean answered Mason's salute and then invited him to take a seat. Mason did so, sitting relaxed but attentive in a high-backed chair that faced the desk.

For a moment Maclean wondered where to start, and then he began quietly to explain about *Vigilant*. He outlined the full story and then detailed his own plans for the destruction of the submarine. Mason listened in silence, gradually absorbing some of the tension that infiltrated through the Intelligence man's words.

When Maclean finished he gave the Marine Captain time to think. Then he said quietly,

"Captain Mason, I want you to lead that strike party on to the Chinese mainland. But I must warn you that you will be entirely on your own if your party is caught by the Chinese. You would undoubtedly be treated as spies and there would be nothing that I could do for you. We think that the attempt stands a good chance of succeeding because the country is so sparsely populated; providing you move only at night and stay hidden during the day there is no reason why you should not reach your objective unseen. However, you just might be unlucky; there are always some factors that can never be foreseen on a job like this." He paused for a moment and then added. "It's a volunteer mission, of course. Nobody outside this room will ever know if you turn it down."

Mason's fingers beat out a tuneless drumming on the edge of the desk and he hesitated thoughtfully. At last he said, "Who else makes up this strike party?"

Maclean said quietly, "Two Marine Sergeants, both of whom have received the same training as yourself. They haven't been asked yet, but I'm hoping they'll volunteer. Their names are Logan and Randell."

Mason looked up. "Not Tom Randell?"

"That's the man."

"A good one too — I'd have picked him myself. I don't think I know this Logan though."

"Perhaps not, but he's another good man; typical brawny Scot and one of the best swimmers in the Marines — and that includes you. Lieutenant-Commander Kendall has also provided two Chinese to guide you, both loyal men."

Mason drummed out another tune and then looked up. "All right, Commander. I'll take the job."

Maclean nodded and said shortly. "I was sure I could rely on you — you were highly recommended." He rose to his feet and crossed to a large chart of the coastline that hung upon the wall. He said quietly, "If you'll step over here, Captain, I'll explain some of the details."

Mason walked over to face the map and Kendall followed him. Maclean used a pointer to indicate the places he named and his listeners followed its stabbing progress across the chart.

"This, Captain, is Choohow Bay where the *Vigilant* was first attacked, by sea it's a good thousand miles to the north of here. And this —" the pointer jabbed again — "is the position from which *Vigilant* sent her last signal; we've christened it Disaster Point. As you can see it's about fifty miles south of Choohow Bay. Now we know from the latest reports sent in by the submarine *Relentless* that there are half a dozen destroyers patrolling a hundred-mile stretch of coastline from Choohow Bay to a spot another fifty miles below Disaster Point. They obviously know she's in the area but they don't know the exact location. Now your party will be landed here —" the pointer tapped crisply at the chart — "at a place called Tung Chu Bay. Tung Chu Bay is eighty miles from Disaster Point, and twenty miles below the patrol area covered by the destroyers.

"Now that eighty-mile march from Tung Chu Bay to Disaster Point isn't going to be a picnic, Captain. You and the other two members of the underwater team will have to carry your aqualungs across your shoulders as well as the explosive charges and the rest of your gear. The two Chinese guides will pack a radio, emergency rations, sleeping bags and everything else needed to make you into a completely self-supporting party. You'll have to travel only at night and you'll have to keep to the hills and avoid anything that remotely resembles a road." He turned to face Mason. "Can you do it?"

Mason was studying the chart. He said slowly, "As you say, it'll be no picnic — but we'll do it."

Maclean said briefly, "Good." He drew another breath and continued. "We've calculated that it should take you five or six days to reach Disaster Point, but it may take more than that due to the rugged terrain. However, even if the Chinese have located *Vigilant* by that time, they won't have had time to start salvage operations. With a bit of luck they might even have her position marked out for you. Either way it will be up to you and the two sergeants to swim down and plant your charges. First you'll use a small charge to smash open the conning tower hatch cover, then you'll enter the submarine and position the main charges. You'll be briefed by an explosives expert before you go, and he'll tell you where to place them for the best effects. All I can tell you is that although the charges are fairly light and compact they are still powerful enough to melt *Vigilant*'s vitals into something resembling a steel blob of half-chewed toffee."

Mason glanced at the chart again and said, "What's the depth, sir? And how far is *Vigilant* from the shore?"

Maclean said grimly. "Working on the assumption that she went down when her last signal broke off we believe her to be about two-and-a-half miles out and under approximately 240 feet of water."

Mason's features tightened. "That's pretty damned deep for aqualung operations."

"I know, Captain, but aqualungs have been used down to 300 feet and it should be possible."

"Maybe, but dives to that depth are mostly brief descents for exploration purposes, and even with the most skilful divers any attempt at physical exertion can be dangerous."

"It is a dangerous depth, Captain, I'll admit that. But you and your men are all experts, you're the best we've got. It will be a tough job, but if it can be done at all then you and your men are the ones most likely to succeed."

Mason shrugged. "All right, Commander. If you say it's possible — we'll do it."

Maclean's face was hard. "I'm depending on you, you're the only hope we have." He turned back to the chart and went on. "After you've done the job you'll have to make your way back to Tung Chu Bay where you can be picked up again. You can bury your underwater gear, or else sink it in the sea, so you'll be able to travel light. Providing everything goes well the Chinese will probably assume that the underwater explosion from *Vigilant* was due to natural causes — her nuclear reactor running wild and overheating, or something like that. Unless they have any other cause for doubt it is highly unlikely that they will suspect the truth."

"And if they do have cause to doubt?"

"Then your party won't have a hope in hell of getting away. If the Chinese realise that there's a landing party of saboteurs skulking around the hills they'll move thousands of troops into the area to hunt you down. And once you're captured we will have to disown you, or at least pretend that you're operating without any proper Naval authority."

Mason grinned suddenly. "In that case I'll try not to get caught."

The night was cold and clear, the stars glittering like points of ice in the black sky. The sea slapped menacingly against the clumsy, squared hull of the junk *Black Lotus*, and the great patchwork sail creaked gently in the wind. The junk smelt highly of fish and its very presence seemed to taint the air around it. Like some grounded bird with one stiffly fluttering wing she slid across the dark surface of the sea towards the rugged land mass of the north China coast that rose slowly from the eastern skyline.

Paul Mason stood in the bows beside the thin, muffled figure of the junk's skipper, a poker-faced Chinese with stained teeth who called himself Captain Kwong. Maclean had sworn of Kwong's loyalty, but Mason failed to find the man's shifty appearance reassuring. He turned his attention to the rapidly nearing coastline and hoped that Maclean was right.

It was three days since the interview in Maclean's office had taken place, and Mason had to admit that when the Intelligence department decided to get things moving it certainly did so with a vengeance. Within a matter of hours the strike party had been formed, thoroughly briefed, and loaded with all their equipment aboard the waiting submarine *Watchful*. *Watchful* had raced north with all possible speed and finally rendezvoused with the *Black Lotus* in the Yellow Sea. The *Black Lotus* had sailed from Shanghai immediately after Maclean's agent in that city had located Kwong in a waterfront bar, and with the aid of her engine and strong winds the junk had been within a hundred miles of Tung Chu Bay when *Watchful* caught up with her. Mason and his party had been swiftly transferred, while *Watchful* submerged to remain within call until she was needed to complete their eventual escape. Now the *Black Lotus* was entering the twelve mile limit of Chinese territorial waters.

Mason watched the skyline as they sailed nearer to the coast, his eyes alert for any signs of a patrolling destroyer. However, the horizon was empty, there was nothing but the black, moving surface of the sea and the soft whispering of the wind in the bamboo-stiffened sail above his head.

Kwong turned to face him and muttered softly. "Get boat ready. No dare go much closer."

Mason nodded and moved back to the stern of the junk where the rest of his party were waiting in the shadow of the high poop. "Get ready with the dinghy," he said quietly.

Sergeant Tom Randell, a tough, stocky man with a confident air of experience, answered him with a brief nod and swiftly began to inflate the rubber dinghy that was to take them on the last lap of their sea journey.

There was silence except for the brief hiss as the dinghy bulged and took shape. The *Black Lotus* moved steadily closer to the black outline of the Chinese hills. There was nothing else to disturb the darkly rippling expanse of the sea.

Slowly the junk began to turn in a slow half circle. As she turned she lost the benefit of the following wind and the great square sail began to sag. Kwong kept her on her curving course until she had drifted almost to a stop. Then he handed the helm to a member of his crew and moved aft to where Mason and his party were waiting.

"You go now, Captain," he said nervously.

Mason nodded. "Okay, Skipper, we'll get out of your hair."

Swiftly and efficiently the dinghy was launched over the side. Randell swung down into the bobbing craft and took the three sets of aqualung equipment that Mason and Logan handed down to him. The rest of their packs followed and then their two Chinese guides, Fen Liu and Chao Lin, climbed down into the boat. Logan remained on the junk's deck, holding the mooring rope that prevented the dinghy from drifting away while Mason exchanged a last word of thanks with the impatient Captain Kwong.

"We expect to be back in ten days," he said quietly. "You know what to do?"

"Yes, yes, I know. I return in ten days at night. I listen for radio call. If no hear go back to sea and try next night. Now you go. Dangerous to stay."

Mason gripped the Chinese Captain's hand, even though he knew that the gesture was not appreciated. Then he turned and dropped lightly into the dinghy. Fen Liu steadied him as he landed and a few seconds later Hugh Logan joined him. The dinghy immediately began to drift away.

As the distance from the junk grew wider Randell and Logan seized a paddle each and began to hurry the dinghy's progress towards the shore. Mason watched the silent shape of the *Black Lotus* for a few moments and then turned his gaze to the land ahead. The paddles splashed very gently as they dipped through the water and the dinghy rolled clumsily on the slight swell.

They were just over a mile from the shore and it took them half an hour of steady paddling to reach Tung Chu Bay. The bay was nothing more than a slight indentation in the rocky coastline and as they approached they could both see and hear the white swirls of foam breaking on the rocks. There was no sign of life as they approached, and the rising hills loomed black and grim above them. Logan and Randell began to paddle more cautiously, for they would need the dinghy again for their escape, and they had no wish to tear out the rubber bottom on the sharp edges of rock.

Behind them the *Black Lotus* still lay silently out to sea, clinging like a great grotesque moth to the horizon. They knew that Kwong could not sail his ship back into the face of the breeze that had brought him inshore, and so he was waiting until they had had time to land safely before starting up his engine to take him out of the twelve mile limit.

The sea hissed and frothed as it broke upon the shore and Mason leaped out into freezing, thigh-deep water in order to check the dinghy mere seconds before she beached. Logan and Randell shipped their paddles and followed him over the side. The two Chinese hesitated for a second and then did likewise.

Carefully the five men manhandled the dinghy through the last few feet of water and up the narrow rock-strewn beach. Mason glanced swiftly around the darkened bay and then ordered them to carry the dinghy and its equipment over to a large clump of boulders nearby. Once they were hidden in the thick shadows at the foot of the boulders they began to unload and then deflate their dinghy.

The sound of an auxiliary engine startled them, carrying with frightening clarity across the sea. They stopped and watched as the distant shape of the *Black Lotus* turned slowly and headed out towards the invisible horizon. Soon she had faded from sight.

Mason said quietly, "Let's get moving and get inland, just in case someone comes to investigate."

The others nodded and quickly set about burying the dinghy in the sand. When the job was done they struggled into the harness of their packs. The clumsy oxygen cylinders of the aqualungs hung heavily across Mason's shoulders; Randell too was panting slightly but the husky Logan seemed quite unconcerned. Fen Liu and Chao Lin were also bowed beneath their heavy packs.

Mason took a wary look around the beach before signalling the others to leave the concealing shadows of the boulders. He led his five-man strike party inland, stumbling and cursing softly as they struggled through the soft sand or half tripped over the rocks. They climbed away from the beach and the now empty blackness of the sea; five ungainly men moving grimly forwards through the night, their efforts concentrated on a mission of sabotage and destruction.

CHAPTER 4: THE BLACK-GLOVED KILLER

While Paul Mason and his small party of volunteers were penetrating inland from Tung Chu Bay on the Chinese mainland Commander Charles Maclean was leaving Naval Headquarters in Victoria and heading his private car through the streets of Hong Kong. The city was ablaze with neon signs that flashed and flickered, lighting up the night sky. The swarming ant-heap of humanity that lived, fought, loved and died in the narrow, jostling streets whirled about him like living debris in a coloured whirlpool of tall white buildings and hanging Chinese banners. Jukeboxes and dance bands were blaring from every café and nightclub, and even from his car Maclean could hear the never-ending rattle of mah-jong chips from practically every building he passed.

Normally Maclean was entranced by the frantic, pulsing life of Hong Kong, marvelling at the sheer speed and vigour of pace at which the Chinese lived. But tonight he had no time to think about Hong Kong; no time to think of anything that was not directly connected with the small group of men he had sent to salvage something from the wreckage of his own mistakes.

Maclean's blunt-jawed face was haggard in the ever-changing glow from the neon lights, and at the moment he was suffering from the old complaint that always gripped him when he had to send a man on a desperate mission; a gnawing sense of uselessness that nagged at his stomach and made him wonder over and over again what right he had to send out a man who might never return. The thought tormented him every time in moments like these. The early planning stages of an operation were all right; as long as he could give orders, make arrangements and double-check safety precautions he could keep the feeling at bay. But once all that had been done and the man who had to actually undertake the mission was on his own, then Maclean's stomach would begin to twist with worry; fearing all the while that there was some factor he had missed that would cost the life of the agent who was obeying his orders.

He thought bitterly that perhaps it would be as well when the storm over *Vigilant* broke in Parliament back home and he was forced to resign his commission. There had been no official protest by the Chinese yet, but there would be as soon as they could locate the submarine and prove beyond doubt her nationality. Then the fat would be in the fire, and he and a few others would be fried with it. Until then, however, he was still Naval Commander in charge of Intelligence, and he had a job to do.

He turned his car into the fast stream of traffic that snarled at suicide pace through Queen Street. Trams clanked noisily past from each direction and he swore in true naval fashion as the sound vibrated through his aching head. He had to swerve abruptly to avoid an indignant pedestrian who scuttled past his bonnet and almost crashed into a wildly-hooting taxi that was pulling out to overtake him.

He was relieved when he was finally able to turn away from the pulsating commercial centre and nose up one of the steep, narrow streets towards the upper levels of Victoria where he lived in a small villa behind the luxury flats that made up the higher class residential area. The noisy throb of Queen Street fell away behind him as the car climbed steadily up towards the lower slopes of the mountains that were flanked with dark-leaved, evergreen shrubs.

As he neared his villa he thought longingly of the stiff drink that he was going to pour himself the moment he arrived, and he began to hunger for a few hours relaxation with his wife and daughter. The thought of relaxing while Paul Mason was taking his risks for him did not seem right, but he tried to push the fact from his mind. There was nothing more that he could do for Mason now.

He reached the neat white villa set in its tiny garden, shadowed with lime and bauhinia trees, and wearily garaged his car. As he walked up to the front of the house the door opened and Fat Lee his Cantonese manservant bowed him politely inside.

Maclean accepted the Chinaman's welcome and gave him his jacket before wandering into the sitting-room. There was no sign of either his daughter, Sheila, or his wife. He sighed and poured himself a large shot of whisky.

The neat spirit left a pool of fire in the pit of his stomach and for a moment the nagging ache that had troubled him was gone. The brief moment of relief tempted him to make a night of it but he decided against it. He poured himself a smaller drink and then put the bottle away.

From the doorway his wife, Elizabeth, said quietly:

"It's been another worrying day, hasn't it?"

He turned to face her. "What makes you say that?"

"I can always tell. On an ordinary night you pour one small drink and it's enough: when you're worried you have to gulp that outsize one first."

He put the glass down and was silent for a moment as he looked into her sadly smiling face.

"I'm a lucky man, Beth. I can't let you understand my work, but at least you can understand me."

She came into the room and kissed him, and for a moment as he held her he felt that he never wanted to let her go. It was strangely wonderful that even after eighteen years she could still arouse that feeling inside him.

He said at last, "Where's Sheila?"

She stayed in his arms as she answered. "She's upstairs, putting on a face." She smiled. "You know what women are, even at seventeen."

For the first time that day he managed to form a smile of his own. "I know — some of them are still the same at forty-two."

She laughed and kissed him again, nuzzling his cheek and then letting her head rest on his shoulder as his hand stroked her hair. She could sense his need for her and she wanted nothing more than to answer it. The demands of her heart dulled her senses for a while, and then suddenly she became aware of the fact that they were being watched.

She lifted her head — and screamed.

Maclean swung round, sweeping his wife's body with him, and for a moment he had a brief glimpse of a grinning face peering through the window behind them. Almost instantly the face vanished.

Maclean let out a bellow of anger and sprang towards the window, but a cry from his wife stopped him. Her face was white with terror and he turned back, compassion fighting with the sudden anger inside him.

The outer door from the garden suddenly burst inwards with a splintering crash, and both Maclean and his wife wheeled to face the sound. The owner of the face they had seen at the window, a tall Chinese in flowing black robes, stood in the open doorway. He was grinning widely and in one hand he gripped a razor-edged hatchet, both the blade and shaft of which had been painted a bright blood red. A second black-robed Chinese appeared behind him and then another scream echoed through the lonely villa.

For the moment Maclean was too chilled to do more than stare in horror, and then the door to the hallway crashed open and Fat Lee stumbled into the room. A look of twisted terror made a ghastly mask of the plump manservant's face and he squealed again before falling face down on the floor. A red-handled hatchet was embedded in the left-hand side of his neck just above the shoulder blade.

The two Chinese in the open doorway yelled hideously and charged into the room. Maclean snapped out of his state of shocked immobility in the same moment and knocked his wife sprawling to the floor out of the way. The next second he dived forward beneath a vicious hatchet swing and tackled the first of his attackers around the knees. The force of the impact carried the man back against his companion and all three went down in a fighting tangle to the floor. Maclean clawed his way up the first man's body, driving knees and fists savagely into the writhing form. The man was gasping in pain, his mouth wide open and showing a range of broken, yellowing teeth. Maclean drove his fist full into the open mouth and felt a crazed sensation of triumph as the tight skin of his knuckles tore against the breaking stumps.

Elizabeth Maclean was struggling to her feet in an effort to go to her husband's aid when another black-robed Chinese came bursting into the room from the hallway. She screamed again as the man jumped over the inert body of the manservant and desperately hurled the whisky bottle from the nearby cabinet into the man's face.

Maclean heard her scream and frantically wriggled free from the two men on the floor. He saw the third man reeling back from the stunning impact of catching a half-full bottle of whisky on the side of his head, and jumping forward he helped the man on his way with a savage blow to the jaw. His first two assailants were already climbing to their feet as he grabbed up a chair and turned to face them. With his free hand he seized Elizabeth by the arm and thrust her into the corner behind him.

The fittest of the two men rushed him, swinging the blunt end of the hatchet at his head. Maclean countered the blow with his chair and kicked the man viciously in the kneecap. The man yelled with agony and staggered away. In the same moment a shrieking scream rang through the higher levels of the house.

"Sheila!" Elizabeth Maclean's face went haggard with horror as she realised that it could only be her daughter.

Maclean took one rushing step towards the hallway and then stopped; torn by a heart-rending decision that no man could have made. His moment of hesitation was his finish for as he stared wretchedly towards the doorway the man whom he had first seen at the window rushed in and aimed a savage blow at the back of his head with the blunt end of a hatchet. Maclean's body arched and stiffened and then crashed heavily to the floor.

His wife uttered a sound that was half scream and half sob, and fell blindly to her knees over his body. The black-robed Chinese grinned as he reversed his hatchet, and then he buried the weapon with one savage blow between her shoulder blades.

The screaming from the upper regions of the house had stopped and a grim silence invaded the house. The three black-robed men stood staring down at the dead woman and the unconscious man who lay among the wreckage of smashed furniture. The man who had murdered Elizabeth Maclean was now holding one hand to his mouth where his broken teeth were beginning to bleed.

There was a sudden movement from outside and all three turned to face the doorway. A tall, thin man stood there surveying the scene, his eyes were hidden behind thick, horn-rimmed glasses and his hands played idly with the silver head of a short cane.

He stepped into the room and another man followed him, a short, chubby man wearing tight gloves of black leather that extended well up his wrists. He was carrying a revolver in one hand. The two men were Dressler and Reutall.

Dressler finished his brief inspection of the room and turned to face the leader of the three Chinese. "Is everyone dead?"

The man nodded. "Two of our number are still upstairs, they have killed the girl and will be searching the rest of the house."

"Right, now get him out to the car." Dressler jabbed his cane towards Maclean's unconscious form. "Hurry."

Two of the Chinese instantly bent over the still form of the Naval Commander and lifted him up. At the same moment there came a sudden scuffle and a squeal from the hallway. An old Chinese woman, the last of the Maclean's servants came running into the room and stopped dead. She stared at the scene before her, her eyes wide with fear in the shrivelled flesh of her face. From behind her they heard the angry yells of the men who had flushed her out of her hiding place.

For brief seconds no one moved. The old woman's hands came up before her in a praying gesture and her lips trembled as she tried to speak. Then Franz Reutall calmly raised the revolver in his black-gloved hand and shot her through the heart.

As the echoes died away Dressler said curtly, "Come on, we must get out of here."

The two Chinese grunted and lifted Maclean up again. Quickly they carried him out of the house. The last two members of the small group of killers came into the room and reported that there was no one left alive in the villa. Dressler hustled them quickly out through the door, and then after a last look round he and Reutall followed. A few seconds later there came the sound of a car disappearing into the night.

As the sound faded one of the bodies on the floor began to stir. Fat Lee was still alive, despite the hideous hatchet wound that had smashed through his collarbone at the base of his neck. He groaned weakly as he tried to reach the side of his dead mistress, and then he fell back, knowing that it was useless. He wondered vaguely what the tong had wanted with his master, for he knew that the men in the flowing black robes with their red-handled hatchets were members of one of the dreaded secret societies that still flourished in the back streets of Hong Kong. Most of all he wondered why the tong men were taking orders from the two Europeans who had been in charge; the tall man with the silver cane, and the little murderer in those strange, tight black gloves.

He fainted again from the sickening smell of his own blood, but the memory of those two men was still stamped clearly in his mind.

CHAPTER 5: ENTER SIMON LARREN

The telephone rang shrilly in the darkness and Rosemary Claydon swore very softly under her breath. The two sounds pulled Simon Larren out of a light sleep and he stirred lazily. The phone shrilled again and the wide double bed creaked as Rosemary shifted her weight. The light clicked on and Larren had to blink his eyes as he looked up at her.

Rosemary Claydon was what Larren had mentally classified as a stray from Debrett. She had rich parents, an unlimited income and a Mayfair flat, and her sole purpose in life was the extraction of its choicest pleasures. At the moment she looked upon Larren as pleasure number one. She smiled at him warmly, her blonde hair slightly tousled by their love-making.

"Damn all telephones," she said. "Who on earth would want to ring at this hour of the morning?"

Larren stretched lazily and slipped one arm around her waist. "Answer it and you'll find out."

She put one finger to her lips in a gesture for silence. "You keep quiet then, and don't tickle while I'm talking."

Larren squeezed her and then closed his eyes and relaxed. The telephone rang yet again and with an elegant shrug of her bare shoulders Rosemary picked it up.

She gave a Mayfair number.

There was the faint sound of an answering voice at the other end and then she cut in sharply. "How dare you? Of course he isn't here. I'm in bed!"

Larren sat up abruptly. "Is that for me?"

"No. No it isn't."

She made an attempt to slam the receiver back on its cradle but Larren grabbed at her wrist.

"Simon you can't answer it. You can't!" Her voice rose hysterically. "Simon, think of the scandal."

Larren said calmly, "To hell with the scandal."

He pulled the receiver from her hand and spoke curtly into the mouthpiece.

"Hello. Larren here."

"Simon — No!" Rosemary made a frantic effort to stop him but his free hand held her at arm's length before she could wrench the telephone from his grasp. She struggled furiously as he listened to the brief, clipped voice at the other end of the line.

"Larren, get out of that woman's bed and get over here right away. I've got a job that needs your personal touch."

The caller had not bothered to identify himself, but to Larren it was unnecessary. There was no mistaking the voice of the little man who called himself simply Mr. Smith.

Larren said flatly, "I'm on my way."

He put the receiver back and looked down at the woman beside him. She had stopped her frantic squirming and now she was almost crying in anger.

"Don't worry," he said, "your reputation is safe. The man who just called has better things to do than to go around spreading scandal."

He released her and she instantly twisted away, turning her back to him and burying her face in the pillows.

"How could you?" she said wretchedly. "How could you give my number to your friends? You're despicable."

Larren was already out of bed and struggling into his clothes. He paused for a moment and then decided that it was pointless to make any attempt at explaining and turned away.

Rosemary suddenly twisted round and sat upright.

"How could you?" she repeated. "You might just as well have sold your story to the Sunday papers." Her voice rose hysterically. "I slept with Rosemary Claydon — that would make a good headline. Why didn't you go all the way and tell them too?"

Larren shrugged his shoulders into his jacket and moved back to the bed. He was a tall man with a hard, unsmiling mouth, and there was something about his grey-green eyes that made Rosemary Claydon shrink back in silence.

He said quietly, "There was only one man who knew that I could be found in your bed if I was needed badly enough, and as I said before, he's not likely to waste time on anything so trivial as your reputation."

Rosemary lunged at him furiously, her fingers spread in an open-handed blow that was partly a slap and partly an attempt to take her nails down the side of his face. The blow caught him on the side of the jaw and drew blood as he jumped back out of the way.

"Get out," she screamed at him. "Get out and don't ever come back."

Larren backed up out of range and gave her a mock bow.

"He who fights and runs away, lives to —"

She snatched up the clock from the bedside table and hurled it at his head. Larren broke off his oratory in time to duck and then put his philosophy into action by making a quick dive for the door.

"You louse," she yelled after him. "You rotten, lousy swine."

Larren slammed the door on her outburst and took a deep breath. He heard the sound of muffled sobbing from inside the room and silently cursed Smith for breaking up a friendship in such a manner. For a moment his conscience pricked him and then he decided that she would soon get over it. Her kind could always love and move on, that was what made them tick.

Without another thought for Rosemary Claydon he hurried down into the street. It was two or three hundred yards to the secluded spot where he had left his white MG sports car and the brief walk in the cold, clean air helped to clear his head. When he reached the car he swung into the low driving seat and headed across London in the direction of Whitehall.

Half an hour later a tireless-looking secretary showed him into a large office in one of the ministry buildings that was only a stone's throw from Parliament Square. The room contained a massive desk and two semi-comfortable chairs. There were no windows and three of the walls were lined with bookshelves. Standing against one wall was a short, plump man wearing a pinstripe suit with a white collar and a dark school tie. His bowler hat was hanging from the stand just inside the door and with it there was a bone-handled umbrella. The little man looked like an ordinary city clerk, a character out of a modern-day Dickens. His name was appropriate to his appearance. He was Mr. Smith.

Smith looked up as Larren entered, and then he calmly replaced the book he had been studying on one of the shelves. The secretary closed the door and Larren waited for the little man to speak.

Smith turned his back to the shelves and said, "Sorry to interrupt your night of debauchery, Larren. I hope the lady wasn't too upset."

The note of mockery made Larren slightly angry and he said curtly. "She was flaming mad. And I can't say I blame her."

Smith moved away from the wall and returned to his desk.

"I'm sorry, Larren. But this is really important." He paused and then asked. "Do the names Dressler and Franz Reutall still mean anything to you?"

Larren looked at him sharply. "You know damned well that they do."

Smith smiled. "Then sit down, Larren, and I'll tell you a story. It seems that your two friends are making mischief again."

Larren took the chair that was indicated to him and Smith seated himself behind the desk. The little man leaned forward and suddenly there was nothing clerk-like in his bearing at all. His grey eyes bored keenly into Larren's face and his tone became that of a man who had long been accustomed to command and responsibility.

"I'll start at the beginning, Larren," he said crisply. "And the beginning is the nuclear submarine *Vigilant* which was sunk a few days ago just off the mainland of China…"

Larren listened with impatient interest until Smith reached the point where Maclean's home had been raided.

Smith said, "…When the police reached Maclean's villa they found one of the servants still alive; a man named Fat Lee. The murderers had obviously left him for dead but he managed to survive long enough to tell the police what had happened. He said that the place had been raided by tong men from one of the secret societies that still thrive in the back alleys of Hong Kong. At one time the tongs were responsible for hundreds of murders every year, but in more recent years the few that still exist operate on a lower scale of extortion and similar crime. However, this dying manservant insisted that the house had been attacked by tong men. He also said that there were two Europeans in charge of the operation: one was a tall, skinny man with thick glasses who carried a silver-headed cane; the other was a little man wearing black leather gloves that stretched far up his wrists who had shot down an old servant woman in cold blood."

Larren's face had become hard and savage. He said tightly, "Dressler and Reutall, it couldn't be anyone else."

Smith nodded in agreement. "I was sure of it too the moment I heard the descriptions. They're a pretty distinctive team."

Larren scowled. "But what the hell are they doing mixed up in a tong murder?"

"Naval Intelligence in Hong Kong don't believe that it is a simple tong murder. For one thing there hasn't been a tong killing in the colony for years; not a ritual killing with the executioners in black robes and using red-handled hatchets anyway. And for another the fact that Maclean was taken away indicates that he's still alive; they wouldn't have any need for a corpse. And thirdly the presence of two top Communist agents makes it pretty clear that the tong men were not obeying motives of their own."

"And you think it's tied up with this *Vigilant* business?"

"Maclean's second-in-command in Hong Kong is sure of it. They've got another submarine still lurking in the area where *Vigilant* went down and they know that the Chinese haven't yet been able to locate her. They think that Maclean was kidnapped so that the other side can force him to reveal her position; as Commander of Naval Intelligence for the area he would obviously be able to tell them all they want to know."

Larren said grimly, "With Dressler and Reutall in the picture they are probably right. We know that Reutall is an expert in the gentle art of torture." He looked straight into Smith's eyes. "Where do I come in?"

Smith said quietly, "You're going to Hong Kong, on temporary loan to Naval Intelligence. You've tangled with those two killers before, you know how they think and you can guess at how they're likely to react to any given situation; that makes you the obvious man for the job."

Larren smiled. "Thanks for remembering me. I was beginning to think I had been forgotten."

Smith ignored him and said, "My secretary has already booked you a seat on the first plane to Hong Kong. It leaves in an hour and a half so you had better get cracking. You'll be working with Maclean's second-in-command, a Lieutenant-Commander named Kendall, and you'll take orders from him."

Larren said thoughtfully, "This is the first I knew that we worked with Naval Intelligence."

Smith smiled. "Normally we have enough problems of our own, but in this case I dug a little deeper when I received an N.I. request for any information on two enemy agents answering to the descriptions of Dressler and Reutall. I saw it as just the excuse I needed to get you out of London before Cedric Claydon had you arrested for the seduction of his daughter."

"Thank you again."

Smith said angrily, "You can dispense with the funny dialogue. Get going and catch that plane."

Larren shrugged apologetically and got to his feet. He was about to turn and leave when Smith added sharply:

"Larren, I seem to remember that Dressler and Reutall were part of the organization that killed your wife. Don't let that fact get in the way of your job. You're going to Hong Kong in order to find Charles Maclean, if he's still alive — not to continue your own vendetta."

Larren turned back to face him. For a moment he was silent and then he said softly:

"Will you have any objection if I take a few days holiday in Hong Kong after this job is completed? I mean after Maclean has been found, and those men on the Chinese mainland have returned safely from their mission."

"For business? Or for pleasure?"

"Pleasure."

Smith said calmly, "No objections, but don't mix the two."

"Thank you, sir."

Larren turned and walked out of the room.

The giant B.O.A.C. airliner dropped through the high bank of white cloud and cruised slowly down towards the island colony of Hong Kong. The brilliant silver-blue of the surrounding sea was scattered with a myriad of smaller islands and was dotted with the moving specks of junks and sampans. The conflicting land and seascape of Victoria and Kowloon was a mixture of wooded hills and tall white skyscrapers, merging back in to the green rice fields of the New Territories and the dim blue hills of Communist China.

Simon Larren stared through one of the thick glass windows of the airliner, but he was unable to assimilate the wondering murmurs of appreciation that came from the other passengers who were seeing Hong Kong for the first time. Larren had other things to think about and he was not here to stare at the scenery.

Simon Larren was a killer; a man who had learned his trade by knifing German sentries in occupied Holland during the Second World War. In the years that followed the war he had quit the espionage business and had eventually married. He had never been able to love a woman before he had met Andrea;

he had adored her and now he knew he could never love another. It was his wife's death that had plunged him back into the grim waters of international espionage that were controlled by men like the unassuming Mr. Smith. Andrea Larren had been killed by a clumsy mistake on the part of an enemy spy-ring, and Larren had tracked down and killed two of the four people who had formed the brains of the group. The other two, the man called Dressler and Franz Reutall had escaped. Since then Larren had lived only for the day when their paths would cross again and he could continue his dark and bloody vendetta.

The airliner began to descend lower over the rising skyscrapers towards Kai Tak airport at Kowloon, and the stewardess began quietly ordering the passengers to fasten their safety belts. Larren clipped on the buckle of his belt as he watched the sprawling twin cities flash below him. On the hill slopes behind Kowloon the military-style tenement flats and the crumbling shacks and lean-tos of the refugee colonies made a pathetic contrast to the atmosphere of prosperity around the gleaming buildings on the seafront. Then the great, broad runway of Kai Tak that stretched far out into the blue waters of the bay was coming up to meet them. The airliner touched down with hardly a bump and taxied slowly to a halt.

Larren followed his fellow passengers into the airport buildings and passed patiently through the various formalities. Once clear he picked up his single suitcase and was about to leave when a tall young man with a purposeful manner came towards him.

"Mr. Simon Larren?" he asked crisply.

Larren kept a blank face. "A mistake I think," he said. "My name is Jones — Percival Sebastian Jones. I'm looking for my Uncle Horace who was supposed to be meeting me here."

The stranger smiled. "Then I'm your Uncle Horace." He reached into his inside jacket pocket and brought out a small identity wallet with a Naval crest. He held the wallet out and added, "I'm Alan Kendall, Lieutenant-Commander attached to Naval Intelligence."

Larren gave him a brief smile of apology. "In that case it's my mistake. I'm too cautious."

Kendall gripped his hand in a short greeting and said. "You can never be too cautious. I have a car outside."

Larren picked up his case and followed the Navy man out of the airport to a sleek black car that was waiting for them with a plain clothes driver.

As the car pulled away a ragged young Chinese man stepped out from a nearby doorway and watched it go. He followed it until it was out of sight and then hurried down the street until he came to a café. He went inside and after a few muttered words with the proprietor he moved over to the telephone and dialled a number.

The sound of the telephone penetrated into the musty interior of the black-draped room where Charles Maclean lay bound and gagged upon the floor. The three men who were standing over the Naval Commander's body looked up sharply. The Chinese man with dark, shining hair and gold-filled teeth said quietly:

"I will go."

"No." Dressler was sick of the smell of burning incense that filled the room, and for the moment he had had enough of watching Reutall trying to make Maclean talk. "I'll get it myself, Cheng."

He left the tong temple and went back into the wide living-room where there was clean air and bright daylight from the windows. He breathed deeply for a minute or two and then turned angrily to the still ringing telephone on the nearby table.

"Who is it?" he demanded in a waspish, hissing tone.

The man at the other end began talking and slowly the anger faded from Dressler's face. When he finally replaced the phone on its cradle he was smiling broadly.

He went back into the temple through the camouflaged door behind the tall curtains that hung down from the ceiling over one wall. Reutall and Cheng looked at him expectantly as he came in.

He said thoughtfully. "That was an interesting call, from one of your tong men, Cheng. He was at the airport when he saw Kendall, the Naval Intelligence man, meet a stranger off the London plane."

He turned to look at Reutall and went on. "Cheng's man gave me a very good description. He said that the stranger was tall with dark hair and wearing a dark grey suit. He had, to quote the man's exact words, a very hard face, and he did not smile. But the most noticeable thing about this stranger was his eyes, they were a strange grey-green colour. Our informer says they were a killer's eyes — like the eyes of a man he knew who was hanged for murder." He smiled. "Who does that description remind you of, Franz?"

Reutall said softly, "A hard-faced man who does not smile, with the grey-green eyes of a killer — could it be Simon Larren?"

Dressler laughed. "The very man I thought of. If it isn't Larren then he must have a double."

The sadistic streak in Reutall's make-up showed in the vicious set of his face. "If it is Larren, perhaps fate will be kind enough to lead him to us. I would welcome another chance to kill Simon Larren — and this time there will be no mistakes."

CHAPTER 6: AT THE SIGN OF THE SCARLET DRAGON

Maclean's secretary gave Larren and Kendall a brief nod as they walked past her and entered the missing Naval Commander's office. Kendall pulled off his jacket with a sigh of relief, for the temperature was somewhere in the upper eighties, and he threw it neatly on to the stand by the door. He moved towards the big desk and then hesitated. He turned to face Larren.

"I hate sitting in the Old Man's chair," he said. "It doesn't seem right somehow. It's as though by taking his place I've already given him up for dead."

"Can you be sure that he isn't?"

"I can't be positive but I'm pretty sure," Kendall compromised by sitting on the edge of Maclean's desk and gestured towards the spare chair. He went on, "Make yourself at home, Larren, and I'll bring you up to date on all the known facts."

Larren accepted the invitation and waited.

Kendall began. "I'll start with the situation regarding *Vigilant*. From the latest report from the submarine *Watchful*, which has now relieved *Relentless* in the area, we know that the Chinese still haven't located the wreck; their destroyers are still searching the whole area. Now that seems to indicate that *Vigilant* came to grief from some internal explosion rather than from a second Chinese attack; otherwise they would be able to concentrate their search. In fact her last signal did say that the Engineering Officer had some cause to fear an explosion. My own theory is that the Chinese must have intercepted part of that last signal that *Vigilant* made to *Relentless*, not enough to give them her position but enough to tell them that she's still somewhere in their waters. They wouldn't know how badly she was crippled, or how fast she was capable of moving under the surface, so they have no idea of how many miles she could have covered between the time of breaking away from their attack and the time they picked up part of her signal."

Larren said thoughtfully, "How long have they been searching now?"

"This is the sixth day since she went down."

Larren frowned and said, "If they're searching systematically they must be getting close to her, so why would they take the colossal risk of kidnapping the head of Naval Intelligence and murdering his household?"

Kendall smiled grimly. "For one thing they're covering a hundred miles of coastline, and as their territorial limits extend for twelve miles that makes one thousand two hundred square miles of sea they've got to search; so they have no reason to hope that they're getting close. And another reason is that they know we must be as keen to see the sub destroyed as they are to salvage her. They can't possibly know that we have a sabotage party on the mainland, but they do know that the longer they take to find her, the more chance we will have of getting there first."

"So it's vital that Maclean is found before they force him to reveal *Vigilant*'s actual position?"

Kendall shook his head. "No, it's not just that. It really wouldn't matter if *Vigilant* has already been located, because by the time the Chinese could get salvage operations organised Mason would have already reached Disaster Point. Even with a few surface vessels stationed up top Mason could still take his party down and plant the charges. In fact we rather hopefully told Mason that with luck the Chinese might even have the sub marked out for him by the time he got there."

Kendall paused for a moment and then finished slowly. "My real worry is that Maclean's kidnappers may not be satisfied with just the position; they may force him to reveal the measures we are taking to make sure that *Vigilant*'s secrets don't fall into Communist hands. And if the reds once begin to suspect that we have a party on the mainland, then Mason and his men can be written off as lost."

Larren said quietly, "What sort of man is Maclean? Will he talk?"

Kendall hesitated, he was obviously reluctant to pass an opinion on the man he respected as a friend. At last he looked up and said:

"Maclean will last as long as any man could be expected to — but we all know that there are limits." He hesitated again and then added, "There is one thing in his favour — he must realise that his wife and daughter are already dead. They can't get at him from that angle."

Larren got up to stretch his limbs and moved over to the window. He stared out for a moment and then turned to face Kendall who was still sitting silently on the edge of the desk.

He said, "One thing I can't understand is why it was necessary to massacre Maclean's whole family and servants. And how do these mysterious tong men fit into the picture?"

Kendall said grimly, "It puzzled me too until the police began trying to investigate. The whole stinking underworld has gone totally deaf, blind and dumb. Nobody saw anything, nobody has heard anything, and nobody is talking. The police have tried every source of information they have but the best they can report are a few veiled warnings to leave the case alone. Nobody will inform on a tong killing — especially this kind. It's quite clear now that the whole household was slaughtered to ensure that the police get absolutely no co-operation from the general public. Even neighbours who must have heard the screaming insist that they were either asleep or away from home and so heard nothing."

"I see. How much do we know about these tongs?"

Kendall shrugged. "These secret societies are practically traditional in China. At one time they wielded a tremendous amount of power and were very highly organised. Their motives were a mixture of politics and religion and they thrived on blackmail, extortion and murder. They controlled their members through sheer terror, and anyone who fell out of line was liable to find himself the subject of a gruesome ritual killing. The tong executioners always left some sign to identify themselves; such as cutting off the corpse's nose or ears, or killing in some special way.

"That of course was years ago; the British have long since broken the hold of the tongs and driven them underground, but they haven't been stamped out altogether. At the present time they are more like any other bunch of criminally-minded thugs who are trying to make a living from blackmail and extortion. They still call themselves tongs and occasionally pass death sentences on informers, but their activities are mostly restricted to the back alleys and the slums."

"And what of this particular tong? How much do you know about them?"

"Well, if they were actually tong men then they're a revival of the old Red Hatchet Tong, which was one of the worst. Their executioners always wore flowing black robes and carried out their death sentences with a short hatchet that was painted blood red. They always left the hatchet in the body as a sign of their identity. We haven't heard of the Red Hatchet Tong for a long time, and in fact this is the first full-dress ritual killing we've heard of for several years. Personally I don't think there is a Red Hatchet Tong any more; my opinion is that the men who raided Maclean's home simply put on a show to frighten the local Chinese. Old fears and superstitions take a long time to die, Larren, and the terror of the tongs was very deep-rooted before they were smashed. Our Communist friends simply decided to play those fears to their own advantage."

Larren said thoughtfully, "Considering that Dressler and Reutall are at the back of it you are probably right. Those two were always reluctant to sail under their own colours. When they had my wife and another man murdered in Paris a few years back they hired a couple of Algerians to do the job. They managed to fool the French Police into blaming the Algerian Nationalists and covered their own tracks completely."

"What else can you tell me about them?" Kendall asked.

"Not a great lot, unfortunately. They were running a spy-ring in London — that's where I first tangled with them — but when it was broken up they escaped behind the Iron Curtain. Franz Reutall, the short, chubby one is a pretty vicious little sadist. He was a member of Hitler's S.S. in Berlin, and a couple of his prisoners turned the tables on him when a shell wrecked his headquarters in the closing stages of the war. His prisoners had good cause to hate him and the story goes that they strapped him to his own desk and then castrated him with a red hot iron. Afterwards they burned the letters S.S. into the back of each of his wrists, which is why he always wears those long black gloves to cover the scars. He was rescued by the Russians before his torturers could go any farther."

Kendall grimaced. "That was pretty ghastly treatment."

Larren shrugged. "Don't waste any sympathy, from what I know of Reutall he deserved a lot more. And he's the one who will take on the job of getting your boss to talk."

Kendall's lips tightened. He said curtly, "What about the other one."

"You mean Dressler — if anything he's more dangerous than Franz Reutall. I don't know his history, and I don't know of anyone who does. Nobody even seems to know whether he has a first name, he simply calls himself Dressler. He has about as much emotion as a dead snake and he operates more like a machine than a man. He's totally dedicated to his cause, and he's the leader of the two."

"An ugly combination."

"Very ugly."

Kendall straightened up and said, "Well, we seem to have covered everything, you now know as much as I do and vice versa. So, what do we do now?"

"I take it that the police haven't made any progress whatsoever?"

"None at all."

"So it seems that there's not a lot of point in pursuing this tong angle. That means we'll have to try another approach." Larren turned away thoughtfully and wrinkled his brows. At last he turned back and said, "There must be other agents of the Chinese operating in Hong Kong, and Dressler and Reutall must be using some of them as contacts. We might get a lead there."

"There are others all right; some we're pretty sure are working against us and some we only suspect, but we won't get anywhere with them. They'll be as close-mouthed as the rest of the underworld."

"To you, maybe. If you know them then they undoubtedly know you. But I'm a stranger here, nobody knows me as a British agent and I just might get results."

Kendall looked doubtful, then he said, "There's nothing to stop us trying. I can give you a list of half a dozen people who are known to be active Communist sympathisers, there may be a link there somewhere."

Larren said briskly, "Right, we'll start with them. It's one line we can follow until we can get something really definite to go on. Even if we get nowhere it will be better than wasting time."

Kendall stood up from the desk and then buzzed for the secretary in the outer office and asked her to bring in the files relating to all known Communist agents and sources of information. There was a few moments delay before the secretary entered with the files and placed them on the desk. Larren moved closer as Kendall started to examine the files.

Kendall said grimly, "There's a junk skipper who operates from Aberdeen fishing harbour and we're pretty sure he works for the reds but we can't prove it. There's also a dancer in a nightclub called the Scarlet Dragon in Kowloon whom we've had cause to watch just lately. There's a work's manager in the dockyards who does a lot of agitating on the sly, and there's a University teacher who's just a bit too clever for us at the moment. There's a businessman who deals in textiles and a financier with a finger in too many pies for his own good. You can take your pick — they're all possibles."

Larren studied the list thoughtfully. At last he said, "Let's try the most obvious approach. It's sometimes a mistake to try and be too subtle. I can't think of any method of becoming acquainted with a financier, or any of the others in that bracket; but any man can try and pick up a dancing girl without arousing suspicion."

"You mean the one at the Scarlet Dragon." Kendal turned a few pages in the file and produced a photograph of a young Chinese woman with slanting brows and a broad smile. He said, "That's her, she calls herself Nancy Kang, she does a bit of singing as well as dancing. The Scarlet Dragon is pretty popular with a lot of young officers and men from the liberty ships in the harbour. If they're drunk enough Nancy lets them buy her drinks and in turn listens to their troubles — and anything else they care to tell her."

Larren gave one of his rare smiles. "Perhaps she'd care to listen to my troubles. How do I find this Scarlet Dragon Club?"

"It's in the Wan Chai area of Kowloon; but be careful, it's an area where you can very easily get your head cracked; it's even possible to get your throat slit."

Larren grinned. "I'm always careful, I have a very hard head, and I promise to keep my chin tucked down and my collar turned up."

There was a certain sleaziness about the neon maelstrom of the Wan Chai area, the narrow streets between the shabby tenement buildings seemed vaguely sinister beneath the blanketing throb of ear-splitting bands and jukeboxes that blared up into the night. Larren paid off his taxi and stood for a minute to watch the roaring river of flesh and steel that surged around the clanging trams along the main street. The neon lights flickered wildly over the hanging Chinese banners with their strange characters and coloured backgrounds, pulsing as though the glass tubes were filled with strains of strange, contrasting hues of live blood.

Larren turned and began to search for the Scarlet Dragon. There were many bars in the area, The Cactus, The New York,

The Honolulu, The Great Shanghai and innumerable others, and it took him some time to find the one he wanted. Wan Chai was the sailor town of Kowloon and he passed dozens of British and American Naval ratings as he searched. Ponytailed women sat in twos and threes at the café and bar-room tables and studied the streets as they waited to be picked up. Larren pushed his way through the jostling throng on the pavements until he found the place he wanted.

A large fire-breathing dragon in scarlet neon illuminated the narrow doorway and Larren paused for a moment before going in. A dance band was blaring from inside and he could hear the sound of mah-jong chips being shuffled by eager hands.

As he hesitated a voice near his ear said earnestly:

"You want better place? Nice film show. Velly cheap."

Larren turned and the pimp who had sidled up to his shoulder took a step back. Larren said gently:

"Go away, before the garbage man comes round and sees you."

Ignoring the man's reaction he entered the nightclub. It was a lot larger than it appeared from the outside, and the atmosphere was hot and close. On his left a long bar ran the full length of the room and to the right there was a small, raised dais where a gaily-dressed combo sweated and blasted the air with tuneless music. Dark, shadowy alcoves lined both walls and were dimly lit by small red lights. The place was crowded and there were a few couples on the small section of the floor that was reserved for dancing. Chinese lanterns hung from the roof and the chairs and tables were all constructed from bamboo. Bright scarlet dragons were breathing orange fire over the background of black velvet drapes that hung from the walls.

Larren let his eyes rove around the impressive interior of the room for a few moments and then moved over to the bar. A white-coated Chinese waiter came to serve him and he ordered a whisky and soda.

While the drink was being poured he turned to face the combo. A dark-haired Chinese woman in a slinky dress of red silk was then stepping up on to the dais and the dancers were drifting back to their tables. The woman on the dais had slanted eyebrows and a big smile. Her dress rose to a high collar that fastened close about her slim throat, but her arms were bare and the dress was split almost to the hip on one side. The combo struck up again and the woman began to sing in a soft throaty voice. Larren recognised her from Kendall's photograph as Nancy Kang.

A slight cough from the Chinese waiter told him that his drink was served and he turned to pay for it. He found himself looking into the soft, liquid eyes of another dark-haired woman in a thigh-baring dress. She laid one hand very lightly on his arm and smiled:

"Would you like to buy me a drink, sir?"

There was something surprisingly naive in both her smile and her voice, and for a moment Larren hesitated. The dark eyes and moist red lips exerted a disquieting charm. Then the waiter said with smiling bluntness:

"It is custom, sir. Most men buy hostess one little drink."

Larren shrugged and decided that he would create less attention by buying the woman a drink than he would be by sending her away. He said casually:

"Give her whatever she's drinking."

The barman nodded and turned away. The woman enlarged her smile and stood a little closer to Larren's side. Her fingers still rested on his arm.

"How you like Scarlet Dragon?" she asked.

"Well, it's certainly got something that the Salvation Army lacks."

Larren paid for the drinks and was aware of her naked thigh pressing against his leg. She was standing very close and he deliberately moved back a pace. He wasn't wearing a shoulder holster because he didn't like them unless they were really necessary — they made an uncomfortable weight and their presence meant that you could never remove your jacket or even allow it to hang open in public — but he did have a sheath knife concealed inside his jacket and he didn't want her to feel it as she pressed against him.

The woman looked slightly vexed but did not push up against him again. She followed his gaze to where Nancy Kang was still singing on the dais; the dancer was swaying to the slow rhythm of the tune and was deftly revealing one long slim leg through the slit in her dress. She sipped her drink and said:

"You think she is better than me?"

Larren looked down and smiled. "I wouldn't say so," he said cautiously. "But I should like to meet her."

The woman by his side pouted her mouth at him and then said:

"Okay. You buy me one more drink, and I ask her to come talk to you."

"It's a deal."

Larren called the waiter over and ordered the same again.

The woman sipped from her glass until Nancy Kang had finished her song and then looked up at Larren.

"You sure it's her you want?"

Larren nodded and after a slight motion of her shoulders she walked away. She had to pass a small table where two more obvious hostesses were sitting alone, but she answered the unspoken question in their glances with a slight shake of her head and they turned resignedly back to their drinks. She vanished through a small door by the dais that had only a moment ago swallowed the slim figure of Nancy Kang.

Larren finished his whisky and waited until he saw the dancer coming towards him. He called to the barman and had a drink ready for her as she reached his side.

She accepted the glass with a smile and said blandly. "Why is it that you want to talk to me?"

"Oh, I just like talking to beautiful women."

"But Marina was a beautiful woman."

Larren smiled. "I'm never satisfied with anything but the best."

She laughed softly and her eyes regarded him with amusement over the top of her glass. They were large, liquid eyes, similar to Marina's except that the slanting brows above them gave her a slightly devilish look. She said suddenly:

"You are not a sailor, and somehow you do not look like a tourist. What are you?"

"I'm a television scout — I'm looking for lovely women with talent."

There was a teasing gleam in her eyes. "What sort of talent?"

"Oh, there are many kinds of talent."

"Perhaps you would like me to demonstrate some of mine."

Larren sipped thoughtfully at his whisky. "It would be an interesting proposition. How about another drink while I give it some thought?"

She accepted gracefully and stayed talking with him against the bar. Larren made no attempt to pump her but concentrated on acting the part of a stray wolf with no other aims except that of taking her to bed. He doubted whether the stuff she was drinking was alcoholic at all, and he had no intention of arousing her suspicions while she was stone-cold sober.

However, after half an hour she put her glass down on the bar and shook her head at his offer of another.

"No," she said. "I have already spent too much time with you. I must go and dance and sing another song or I shall lose my job." She flashed him a smile and moved quickly away.

Larren let her go and watched the sinuous movement of her hips as she zig-zagged deftly through the close cluster of tables towards the stage. He smiled to himself at the exaggerated wriggle and then picked up his glass.

A few moments later Nancy Kang began to sing again, crooning a husky love song into the microphone in defiance to the shattering backing of the combo. As she sang her eyes roved over the heads of the crowd until her gaze settled on Larren's face. He smiled and raised his glass.

He decided that his best course now was to take a seat and wait for her to finish her song and rejoin him, and glass in hand he made his way towards the nearest table. He failed to notice the neatly-dressed Chinese with the golden teeth until the man stepped into his path.

"Excuse me, Mr. Larren. I must talk with you."

The man's sudden appearance and polite tone caused Larren to halt in surprise. For a moment his mind was too busy to answer as he wondered how on earth the man could have known his name. Except for Naval Intelligence there was no one who knew of his presence in Hong Kong, and he decided that the man must be connected in some way with Kendall.

The Chinese raised both hands in an expressive gesture and rested them lightly on Larren's arms.

"It is very important, Mr. Larren. Very important."

Larren smiled and was about to brush aside the man's restraining hands before answering when abruptly the lights went out and the club was plunged into total darkness. Instantly the hands of the polite-voiced stranger clamped savagely on Larren's arms, and the Britisher knew for certain that the man was not from Alan Kendall.

Instinctively Larren dropped to his knees and even as he fell he felt a heavy body blunder into him from behind. There was a brief scuffle and the sickening sound of a blow, and then the man who had tried to detain Larren fell backwards with a shrieking scream. Larren rolled desperately to one side.

He heard the crash of the gold-toothed man's falling body and then the sound of running feet. His hand slipped into the inside pocket of his jacket as he rolled to his knees and he closed his fingers over the hilt of the razor-edged sheath knife that was concealed in the coat lining.

The knife was his favourite weapon, and in the darkness one that he preferred to any automatic. A gun released a loud crack that could draw a retaliating shot, but in the hands of an expert a knife killed silently. This particular knife was his only souvenir of the distant days of the war, and the blade had been baptised in blood on his first mission for the organisation known as S.O.E. Now he drew it clear and transferred it to his right hand with one easy movement, staying utterly silent as he crouched and waited. Around him the pitch blackness of the Scarlet Dragon was in an uproar, tables were crashing over, men were shouting and women were screaming.

Then abruptly the lights came on again.

A few feet from where Larren crouched the gold-toothed Chinese was spread-eagled on his back on the floor. The red-handled hatchet that had been meant for the back of Larren's skull was embedded in the Chinaman's forehead just above and between the eyes.

His killer had vanished.

CHAPTER 7: SNARED BY A SMILE

For A few brief seconds there was a shocked silence in the Scarlet Dragon; the customers stared dumbly at the crouching figure of Simon Larren and the sprawling corpse on the floor. The dim red lights above the curtained alcoves around the walls gave a hellish glow to the scene and abruptly a woman found her voice and uttered a shrill scream of horror before tumbling to the floor in a dead faint. The sound gave life and movement to the shock-frozen faces that filled the room and there was pandemonium as the customers stampeded for the exits. Glasses were smashed and spilled and the frail bamboo tables and chairs were overturned or hurled aside as frantic men and women fought to reach the street. Several women screamed but the sounds were lost in the general uproar. The sight of that ugly red hatchet that had smashed into the gold-toothed man's forehead had spread terror faster than anything Larren had ever seen before, and the dreaded name of the tong was sweeping through the crowd on a wave of fear.

Larren straightened up and looked towards the dais where Nancy Kang had been singing. The musicians on the small stage were still gaping with startled faces, but of the slim Chinese woman in the slit red dress there was no sign.

Larren realised that he would never catch the dancer now. She already had a good start on him and by the time he could force a passage through the panic-stricken crowd she would be lost in the streets outside. The unseen killer had also escaped while the lights were out, and that left Larren with only one line to follow up — the dead man at his feet.

Swiftly he slipped his knife back into the sheath that was sewn into the lining of his jacket, and then he knelt down beside the body. Deftly he went through the man's pockets but he could find no clue of identification. The man did not even carry a wallet. Baffled, Larren glanced around, and then he saw the barman staring at the scene from behind the counter. The man looked into his face and then suddenly turned and bolted. Larren realised that if the dead man was a regular customer then the barman would be sure to know something about him, and without hesitation he took a short, running jump and a spring that carried him clean over the bar.

The barman looked back as Larren landed with a crash that sent a tray of glasses flying to the floor. His eyes widened with alarm and he made a desperate attempt to get through the narrow door at the back of the bar before Larren's hand grabbed at his shoulder.

Larren spun the man round to face him and clamped both hands on the white lapels of his jacket. The man's mouth was grotesquely slack and trembling and his eyes bulged fearfully as he struggled in Larren's grasp.

Larren said tightly:

"That man on the floor — is he a regular customer?"

The barman choked and Larren shook him violently.

"Is he a regular customer?"

"Yes. Yes he come often." The man's voice was high and shrill. His gaze desperately searched the club room on the other side of the bar but the place was still in chaos and nobody was taking any notice of his plight. He went on in anguish.

"You let me go now? Please. Please."

"If lie's a regular customer then you'll know his name?"

"No." The word was a shriek. "Not know nothing. Please."

Larren's grey-green eyes were hard and vicious.

"I want his name."

"I don't know. I swear I know nothing. I swear."

Larren's mouth became a vicious slit across his face. He swung the man round in a half circle that pulled him off his feet, his body sagging and his heels kicking helplessly at the floor.

"I want that man's name," he said savagely.

"No. Tong kill me. Tong kill me." The man was literally slavering and his distended eyeballs seemed on the point of bursting. His struggles were becoming pathetically weaker.

Larren released the barman's coat with one hand and deliberately closed his fingers around the man's windpipe. He squeezed with slowly increasing pressure as the wretch choked and writhed in his grasp. When he stopped the man's face was sickly and his breath was rasping harshly in his throat.

Larren said softly, "All I want is his name."

The barman was sobbing for breath. "He is — he is Cheng Kia." He blurted at last. "Tong will kill me." he added miserably. "Tong will kill me."

"To hell with the tong. Where does this Cheng Kia live?"

"He has a big house outside Kowloon. He is a very rich man."

"Where outside Kowloon?"

The barman was resigned to his fate now. He said dully, "Place called Tolong Bay. Very big house." He looked beseechingly into Larren's face. "That all I know. I swear."

Larren pulled the man upright and then let him go; he had learned all he wanted to know. Apart from themselves and the grim corpse on the floor the Scarlet Dragon was now empty. A brooding silence had settled over the wreckage of the smashed furniture, but from somewhere outside came the shrill sound of a police whistle.

Larren realised that it was time that he got out; he had things to do and no time to waste answering police questions. If the police caught him he would be delayed while they contacted Naval Intelligence to vouch for him, and it was imperative that he reached Cheng Kia's home immediately. He knew that Cheng must have been an accomplice in the attempt to murder him, and it was only by luck that he had been able to duck down and avoid getting that red-handled hatchet in the back of his own skull. Even now he could taste the dryness of fear that had filled his mouth as Cheng's hesitant hands had gripped him firmly in the sudden darkness; and he knew that Cheng's task had been to hold him still in the brief seconds while the killer struck, then they would have both slipped away before the lights came on again. But the attempt had failed; Cheng Kia was dead, and provided that Larren moved fast there was just a chance that he could pick up something useful at the dead man's home.

Without another thought for the trembling barman Larren turned and hurried out of the club. A large crowd had gathered on the pavement outside, but they kept their distance and merely gaped at him as he came through the door. Farther up the road a Chinese policeman was puffing wildly into his whistle and thrusting his way into the crowd. Larren's mind registered the scene at a glance and then he quickly pushed his way through the crowd, moving in the opposite direction to the oncoming policeman. No one in the crowd made any attempt to detain him and he hurriedly lost himself in the sea of humanity that swirled through the streets. An empty taxi came towards him and he stepped off the pavement to flag it down. It stopped with a screech of brakes and instantly Larren swung inside. Without waiting for directions the young Chinese at the wheel put his foot down and the taxi roared off again.

The driver neatly steered between two dodging pedestrians crossing the road and then looked back over his shoulder, his teeth showing in a wide grin.

"Where to, Johnny? Nice girls? Film show?"

Larren said grimly. "How long will it take you to drive out to Tolong Bay?"

The Chinese shrugged. "Half an hour — maybe."

"Make it in twenty minutes and I'll pay you three times the fare — if you don't I'll bang your head through the windscreen."

The driver looked startled and then he grinned again.

"You said it, Johnny."

His foot pressed down and the taxi leaped forward like a rearing stallion. Larren leaned back and tried to relax.

While the taxi charged through the wide chasms of light and feverishly rushing traffic that made up the main streets of Kowloon, Larren began to arrange the incidents at the Scarlet Dragon into logical order in his brain. He couldn't quite remember whether he had seen Cheng Kia when he first entered the club or not, but somehow he didn't think that the man had been present then. He seemed to remember the man standing near the door while he was talking to Nancy Kang, but again he couldn't be sure; it was always difficult to think back to things that had had no importance at the time.

He changed the subject of his thoughts and concentrated on Nancy Kang. The dancer had vanished well before the lights went on again, which meant that she had probably known exactly what was happening; and that in turn seemed to indicate that she had had a hand in arranging the murder attempt. During his conversation with her he must have blundered somewhere and she had guessed who he was; then she must have made some sign to the barman or one of the waiters who had promptly sent for Cheng Kia and his unknown accomplice.

The point that really puzzled him was the fact that Cheng Kia had known his name. He had entered Hong Kong with an efficiently faked passport and until Cheng Kia had addressed him he would have sworn that only Alan Kendall and a few of his colleagues knew of his real identity. However, he had to face the facts; somehow Dressler and his comrades had learned that he was in Hong Kong, and they were not hesitating to use messy techniques in trying to kill him.

That Cheng Kia and his accomplice had been sent by Dressler Larren did not doubt for a moment. Cheng Kia had obviously been a tong man, fake or otherwise, and the merciless slaughter of Maclean's household proved that the tong were working hand in hand with Dressler and Reutall. The barman had also said that Cheng Kia was a rich man who lived in a very big house, and it was reasonable to suppose that a man who was rich and influential in one way would also be an influential member of any society to which he belonged. That last thought gave Larren good cause to hope that he might find a new lead at Cheng's home, if not to Dressler at least to the newly-revived Red Hatchet Tong. However he had to get there fast, before Dressler learned of Cheng's death and ordered his minions to erase any clues at the dead man's home.

Larren did his best to restrain his impatience as his taxi honked and screeched its way through the garish streets. At any other time he would probably have been sweating at the suicide fashion in which the young man at the wheel was driving, but at this moment he craved only speed.

They began to pass blocks of shabby tenement flats, built like unattractive stacks of matchboxes with grey, washing-draped balconies. The teeming, neon-lit heart of Kowloon was behind them and the road began to bear left, circling towards the sea. At last the taxi mounted the crest of one of the foothills behind the city and beyond the buildings below was the blackness of the sea, pierced with countless red splashes of light from the night-fishing boats that were scattered over its surface.

The driver looked back and beamed. He held up his wrist and gestured to his watch as he said. "Tolong Bay, Johnny. Eighteen minutes."

Larren said quickly. "Do you know the home of a man called Cheng Kia?"

The Chinese shook his head and his face looked genuinely sad.

Larren pulled out his wallet and extracted a fistful of notes, for he had been well supplied with cash before he had left Naval Headquarters. He said briskly, "Cheng Kia is a very rich man, and he lives in a big house somewhere down there. Find it for me."

"Sure, Johnny."

The Chinese slammed in his clutch and Larren was thrown back into his seat as the taxi rushed down the hill. The grinning driver took a corner on two wheels as he swung into another well-lighted street, and a few minutes later he braked hard before an open café where a jukebox was shrieking into the night. He was out of the taxi almost before the vehicle had stopped and he darted swiftly into the café. Two minutes later he had returned and wriggled back into his seat, his grin broader than ever.

As he pulled away again he said cheerfully. "Like you say, Cheng Kia very rich man — everybody know him. Most helpful."

Larren grinned back at him and said, "You ought to sell this heap and become a detective, you'll make more money and you'll probably live longer."

The man laughed politely as he scorched his protesting tyres around another corner. Then he was heading up the slope of another low foothill that was flanked with scrub and dotted with small villas. One building stood out from the rest, a sprawling, white-painted house that was by far the biggest in the area. Larren's driver pointed his arm and said.

"That the house of Cheng Kia."

Larren separated enough notes to make sure that the man was amply repaid from the roll in his hand, the rest he replaced in his wallet. Leaning forward he paid the driver off and said:

"Drop me about a hundred yards away. I'll walk the rest."

"Sure, Johnny. Sure." He did as he was ordered and pulled the car into the roadside. "You want me to wait, Johnny?"

Larren shook his head. "No, I might be quite a while. Thanks a lot."

The driver saluted and then, after a moment's hesitation, he reversed his vehicle and drove away.

Larren watched him go and then turned to walk the last few yards to the villa. There were lights showing in the big white building, but there were no cars parked outside to indicate any late visitors, and Larren's hopes that he had arrived before any of Dressler's hired tong men grew brighter. He walked up the short, narrow drive to the door and then paused to take a final reconnoitre of his surroundings. Then he carefully smoothed his hands down his thighs in a characteristic gesture that removed the sweat from his palms, and moving forward he calmly pressed the bell beside the door.

He barely had time to step back before the door was pulled open and he found himself facing a small, almost fragile-looking young Chinese woman. She was not much more than twenty years old, and was wearing a high-collared dress of black and gold silk that was clasped tightly to her slim waist by a broad white belt. She wore her blue-black hair in a long ponytail and her dark eyes were shaded by delicate brows. She was smiling but when she saw Larren the smile instantly faded. Her red lips mouthed a startled, almost soundless O and Larren knew that she had been expecting someone else.

He said calmly, "I am looking for Mr. Cheng Kia. Is he at home?"

The young woman's hands moved vaguely, fluttering like slender white swallows. "I am sorry," she said, "Cheng Kia is not at home. I am expecting him though. I thought it was he who was ringing." Her words tumbled over each other in short, nervous sentences.

Larren said blandly, "I have a message for him — from Comrade Dressler."

The woman obviously knew the name for she made no comment. Instead she stepped back and said, "You will wait for him? You must come in."

Larren stepped past her into a wide hallway, and she closed the outer door behind him. She turned quickly to look up at him and said, "My name is Maxine. I am Cheng's sister." She held out her right hand and after a few seconds Larren realised he was expected to shake it.

His own grip almost swallowed her small palm and he had to suppress a smile at the incongruous formality of the gesture. He decided that she had obviously been watching too many

English films and humoured her by remaining solemn. He introduced himself in the name of Mr. A. Simon.

Maxine Kia looked vaguely troubled when Larren relaxed his grip and she pulled her hand away with a sharp jerking movement.

She said, "What is it that you must tell my brother?"

Larren said apologetically. "It was rather personal."

"From Comrade Dressler?"

"That's right."

She hesitated for a moment and then said, "You had better come into the living-room. I will find you a drink."

Larren accepted the invitation and followed her into a large room that was expensively and tastefully furnished. One wall was almost wholly taken up with a wide window that looked out on to the slope of the low hill and the light-speckled blackness of the bay beyond. The opposite wall was draped with tall red curtains. Maxine Kia moved over to a small lacquered table that supported a variety of bottles and glasses, and after a brief query to Larren she poured him a whisky.

Larren took the glass she offered him, deciding that he had successfully allayed any suspicions she might have had and wondering how he could best turn the situation to his advantage.

Maxine watched him drink and then said suddenly:

"You say you come from Dressler — have you come for the papers that Cheng has been keeping for him?"

Larren had no idea of what papers she was talking about, but anything that was important to Dressler was worth following up and he answered blandly, "As a matter of fact that is why I am here. I did not realise that you knew about them."

"Cheng told me," she replied. She hesitated and then went on, "If you wish I can get them for you, I know where they are kept."

Larren finished his drink and replaced the glass on the table. "That's a good idea," he said. "If you can get them now it will save time when Cheng comes."

Maxine nodded and her long ponytail danced a little jig between her shoulder blades with the motion of her head. She moved over to the tall red drapes that curtained off the far wall and pushed them aside to reveal a hidden door. From the wide belt around her waist she extracted a small key which she deftly inserted in the lock. Pulling the door open she held the curtains back so that he could pass through.

"Come," she said. "They are in here."

Larren had to duck low through the secret door as he passed her and instantly the smell of burning incense swept into his nostrils. He found himself standing in a large black-draped room that was dimly lit by sinister, red-shaded lighting. Directly opposite him was a curtained alcove that was reached by three low steps, in front of the alcove was a dark-stained altar and on each side smoking joss sticks released the sickly smell that filled the room. The dark curtains above the altar bore the blood-red emblem of a short hatchet.

Larren realised that he was in a tong temple.

Maxine closed the door and he heard the lock click behind him, and in the same moment he was aware of the fact that they were not alone. A man was standing rigidly in the black shadows to the left of the altar, and even in the dim light Larren could see that he was a massive giant of a creature. His features were those of a Mongol, the cheekbones high and the domed skull completely bald. He was naked but for a loincloth and the huge muscles of his arms and chest rippled beneath a glistening film of sweat.

As he stepped forward into the light Maxine Kia gave Larren a violent push, at the same time tripping his feet to send him sprawling face down on to the temple floor.

She screamed frantically, "Kill him, Kolo. Kill him. Kill him."

CHAPTER 8: VICTORY AND DEFEAT

In the few brief seconds as he fell headlong to the temple floor Larren realised how neatly he had been snared by Maxine's innocent, half-nervous smile. It was abruptly clear now that the mysterious papers she had mentioned were nothing but a non-existent lure to entice him into the temple where the huge guardian could deal with him. Maxine Kia was nowhere near as fragile and un-resourceful as she looked.

The Mongol was already moving forward as Larren fell; his lips were drawn back in a hideously child-like smile that indicated low mental abilities as well as revealing ugly, yellow-stained teeth. His fingers were outstretched as he reached towards Larren and he was more of a lumbering, hairless ape than a man.

Larren managed to break his fall slightly with his palms, and with Maxine's screaming orders to kill still ringing in his ears he rolled clumsily to one side. The Mongol's first rushing lunge missed and Larren came up on to one knee and thrust one hand inside his jacket in an attempt to reach his beloved sheath knife. He was still winded from his fall and the movement was far too slow. The Mongol wheeled on to him instantly with an unbelievable show of speed, one massive hand clamping on his knife wrist and the other clutching at his throat.

Larren choked helplessly as the throttling fingers dug into his flesh just below his chin. The Mongol had stopped grinning and his mouth was closed tightly in an effort of concentration. His eyes were staring and his sweating body gleamed in the dim light. The muscles of his powerful arms swelled and bulged as he held Larren still. Larren's lungs were bursting and his mouth gaped helplessly as he fought for his life. His free hand clawed at the Mongol's wrist.

"Kill him, Kolo. Kill him!" Maxine ordered shrilly.

Larren's vision was veiled by a red mist now and he knew that at any second he must black out. He struggled feverishly in one final bid for life and somehow he managed to straighten up from his knees. Deliberately he allowed his body to sag again and braced the soles of his feet against the Mongol's ankles as he pushed the man's legs apart. The Mongol roared with anger as his feet were forcibly splayed out, and losing his balance he crashed over on his back. He pulled Larren with him as he fell, but as his shoulders hit the floor he had to relax his grip on Larren's throat. Larren used the last of his fading strength to drive his knee with sickening force into the man's groin.

Larren barely knew what he was doing as he rolled away from the Mongol's embrace. He sucked in life-giving air that burned like draughts of fire in his bruised throat, and for the moment he was too dazed to see anything more than the hideous red mist that swam in his brain. More by instinct than intention he stumbled to his feet, but then he had to slump against the nearest wall for support.

The Mongol still writhed on the floor, his body doubled up from that cruel blow to the groin. He snarled in agony through the frantic panting of his breathing and banged his shining skull against the floor in a wild effort to kill the pain. Then suddenly the pain transformed itself into sheer blood-lusting fury and he seemed to throw himself to his feet.

Larren still leaned against the wall, hanging on to one of the black velvet drapes for support. His head still throbbed and his throat burned with pain but some of his strength had ebbed back into his limbs. He heard the roar of the Mongol as the man charged, even though he could still barely see through the tears in his eyes, and desperately he heaved himself up by the velvet drapes and kicked out with both feet. His heels caught the Mongol squarely in the forehead and the giant guardian let out a howl as he toppled back to the floor. In the same moment Larren's weight pulled the heavy curtain down from its fastenings and he too crashed back to the floor with the smothering weight of the curtain on top of him.

For a moment Larren panicked as he fought his way free of the restraining folds, and then sanity came back to him as he struggled clear. The Mongol was facing him on his hands and knees and without hesitation Larren scrambled to his feet and hurled the encumbering curtain over the man's head.

The heavy drape settled perfectly, completely enveloping the enraged guardian of the temple. He reared up with the black velvet still swirling round him and blinding him, and as he struggled in turn to get clear Larren smashed his clubbed fist down on to the back of his neck where the shape of his bullet head showed clearly through the folds.

The Mongol staggered drunkenly, roaring with anger. Savagely Larren struck again and again at the same spot, exerting every last ounce of his strength into the merciless blows. With the last, tremendous blow of his fist the Mongol sagged forwards and fell with a crash, and the swirl of black velvet settled round him like a shroud.

Larren was trembling as he stared down at the muffled body of his opponent, and it was a few seconds before he became aware of Maxine Kia gaping at him from just inside the closed door.

"Kolo," she said slowly, her voice strained and disbelieving. Her dark eyes found Larren's face and she turned and rushed for the door, her fingers fumbling for the key to the lock.

Larren said harshly, "You shouldn't have locked us in. You were too sure of your pet executioner."

She looked round as he approached and then tried to duck past him and run. Larren grabbed at her shoulder and spun her round to face him.

"Don't run away just yet, Miss Kia. I want to know why you were so eager to watch our friend Kolo wringing my neck."

Her eyes were moist with tears of pain and rage. "Cheng will kill you for this," she burst out passionately. "He will send the tong to cut your heart out."

"I doubt it," he retorted coldly. "You see — Cheng Kia is already dead."

The dullness of shock slowly replaced the fury in her eyes. Then she said slowly, "You are lying. You must be lying."

Larren said, "No. I left Cheng Kia's corpse in a nightclub called the Scarlet Dragon just before I came here."

Something in his eyes and the unsmiling line of his mouth told her that he was telling the truth. She looked away from him and her slim body trembled with silent sobbing.

Larren snapped curtly. "Don't bother with arousing my sympathies — I don't have any. Just tell me why you lured me in here so that your tame killer could try tearing me apart with his bare hands?"

She looked up, her expression was rigidly controlled but her eyes were a conflicting mixture of emptiness and pain.

"I knew you were a spy," she said quietly. "You could not have come from Dressler."

"How did you know?"

"By the way you shook my hand." Her tone was dull and uncaring and she went on. "There is a special grip by which the tong men recognise each other. Dressler knows it, and if he had sent you here he would have showed it to you."

She tried to look away but Larren gripped her chin with his free hand and forced her to keep her eyes on his face.

He said softly, "Where is Dressler now?"

The hatred began to kindle in her dark eyes again and she said fiercely, "I do not know, and if I did I would not tell you."

Larren had by now recovered the normal self-confidence that had been battered out of him by his encounter with the giant Mongol, and although his throat was still sore most of the effects had worn off.

He said calmly, "If you can't tell me anything I might as well tie you up while I have a look round." He deftly pulled off his necktie as he spoke and none too gently forced her to the ground. There was a brief struggle before he could secure both her wrists behind her and then he lashed them tightly together. He rolled her over on to her back so that she was looking up at him and remarked calmly:

"There, that should keep you still for a bit."

Maxine twisted helplessly and then said savagely, "There are other tong men besides my brother Cheng. You will still die."

Larren said flatly, "If you don't shut your pretty mouth I'll have to gag it."

Maxine glowered at him but wisely said nothing. Her red lips were clamped hard together and she jerked her head to one side and refused to look at him.

Larren left her and moved over to the shrouded heap of the unconscious Mongol. He pulled the heavy drape away and satisfied himself that the temple's guardian was not likely to recover his senses for some time. He was unable to suppress a shudder as he looked down at the monstrous, hairless hands that had so very nearly choked the life out of him, and as he replaced the heavy drape he half hoped that the man would suffocate.

Without another thought for the Mongol, Larren began to examine the interior of the temple. The white smoke still curled up from the burning joss sticks on either side of the altar and the cloying smell stuck in Larren's throat as he moved closer. The brown stains on the altar looked suspiciously like blood, but as it was only a small affair it seemed most likely that nothing larger than chickens had ever been sacrificed there. Larren hesitated for a moment and looked beyond the altar to the hanging curtains that bore the grim symbol of the red hatchet. The three short steps before the curtains seemed to indicate that there was an opening of some kind behind them. Larren circled round the altar and climbed the low steps. Briskly he pulled the curtains aside.

He found himself facing a small alcove that was recessed into the wall. The alcove was lined with blood-red velvet and standing on a raised dais in the centre was an elaborate throne, each arm of the throne ended in a basin shaped like a cupped hand in which more incense burned in sickly-sweet coils of rising smoke. Larren stared, and then from behind the throne he heard a muffled movement, followed by a slight groaning sound.

Swiftly he stepped up into the alcove and around the throne. He stared down into a narrow hollow behind the raised dais and saw a man lying at his feet. The man was lying on his back with his hands lashed behind him and his ankles bound tightly together. A silk scarf gagged his mouth and his white shirt front was ripped wide open to reveal a darkly-haired chest that was smeared with streaks of dry blood. The man's eyes were wide open and staring above the gag and his hair was streaked with silver at the temples.

Larren knew without doubt that he had found Commander Charles Maclean.

For a brief moment he was filled with elation at having achieved his purpose in coming to Hong Kong, and then the elation faded before the black rage that followed the sight of the blood-smeared marks of torture. Swiftly he dropped down on one knee and fumbled to remove the gag. The silk scarf was pulled hard into Maclean's mouth and was knotted tightly behind his head, and Larren had some difficulty in getting it undone. Once it was free Maclean coughed hoarsely and gulped eagerly at the scented air.

"Who — who are you?" he got out at last.

Larren said grimly, "Don't worry, I'm a friend. The name is Simon Larren. I'm working with a friend of yours named Alan Kendall."

Maclean said hoarsely, "Good for Alan — knew I could rely on him."

In the cramped hollow behind the dais there was little that Larren could do and he hoisted the man out and started to drag him clear of the alcove. Maclean gasped and moaned as Larren lowered him on to the temple floor beside the altar, and Larren forced himself to take his time and treat him more gently.

Maclean licked his lips and said, "Thank God you found me. I don't think I could have held out much longer."

Larren's face hardened. "I suppose Reutall has been trying his little methods of persuasion." Maclean nodded weakly and he went on, "Don't worry, I'll soon have you out."

He reached into his jacket for his knife to cut the ropes that bound Maclean's wrists, and in the same moment he heard a soft swishing sound from the drapes behind the altar. There was the click of a closing door and then a new voice said venomously,

"Don't bother to release the Commander, Larren. It would be a waste of both my time and yours."

Larren froze, knowing that the slightest move could mean his death. Bitterly he cursed the cruel fate that had turned his victory into defeat when just a few more minutes would have sufficed to release Maclean and get him away. He knew without doubt that the hissing, sibilant voice behind him belonged to Dressler.

He let his hands fall away from his jacket and then very slowly turned his head. Behind him and just to one side of the alcove behind the altar the black drapes had been pushed back along the wall. A second exit was now revealed and three men stood facing him with their backs to the door. One was a tall Chinese man, the second was Franz Reutall, and the third, standing with his elegant cane in one hand and an automatic revolver in the other, was Dressler.

Larren said, "I should have guessed that there was a back exit somewhere behind all those drapes; every rat hole always has its avenue of escape."

Dressler came farther into the room, the weird lighting throwing grotesque shadows over his thin, bony face beneath the horn-rimmed glasses he always wore.

"You always were too impatient, Larren," he said. "It is as well that I remembered that when I learned that Cheng Kia was dead. I guessed that you would do the obvious thing and rush over here to Cheng's home."

"So Nancy Kang tipped you off."

"No." Dressler turned slightly and gestured to the Chinese man behind him. "No, it was our friend Tao Shen. Tao is an invaluable man, he was with Cheng at the Golden Dragon — he also helped us to kidnap Maclean." He paused and added, "You remember Franz, of course."

Larren looked past him at the cherubic features of the little sadist. The man was exactly as Larren had last seen him, he was wearing an identical black suit and his hands were covered by the long black leather gloves.

He said, "I remember him."

"I am glad." Reutall's tone was silky. "I am so very glad. I have looked forward to this moment for a long time, and it would be spoiled if you had forgotten."

Dressler walked towards Larren and stood over him where he still knelt by the helpless Maclean. The automatic pointed directly at Larren's temple.

He said, "I am sorry, Larren, but now that old acquaintances have been renewed we must break up the party and leave. The police will no doubt have the same idea as you once their investigation gets under way, and it would be too ironic if I in turn allowed myself to be caught by them." He paused and added, "I hate to do this but it is safer."

In the next second he swung his silver-topped cane in a swift, blinding blow that knocked Larren senseless to the floor.

CHAPTER 9: IN THE SAMPAN JUNGLE

The first sensation that soaked its way into Larren's reeling brain was the fast-swelling ache of pain; pain that spread down from the tender softness of his split skull and radiated from the burning agony of his wrists that were suspended above him. Long before he opened his eyes he knew that he was standing upright and that the main bulk of his weight was supported by his arms which were lashed somewhere above his head. His toes were barely touching the floor and the drag of his body was causing the ropes to cut viciously into his wrists.

At first he could only feel the pain, but eventually his other senses also began to function. His nostrils registered the overall stench of rotting fish, filth and human excrement. There was a background sound of shouts and splashes, shrill voices, squawking fowls and the whining yelp of a dog. He felt an almost imperceptible movement beneath his feet that told him that he was aboard some kind of water craft.

With a determined effort he managed to open his eyes, and despite the rushing surge of pain and sickness he kept them open long enough to record his surroundings. He was alone in a small cramped cabin that was furnished by a crude wooden table and some rough grass matting on the floor. There were no portholes and the only light came through chinks and gaps in the roof above him. The place smelt abominably and was shrouded in dusty twilight despite the fact that it must have been broad daylight outside.

With an effort he craned his head back to look up, the movement thrusting deep probes of pain through his skull. He saw that his wrists were lashed one to each end of a rope that passed over the stout beam that ran along the centre of the deckhead. He had been hoisted up so that even by standing on tiptoe he could not take any real amount of his weight from his wrists. The throbbing in his head caused his chin to drop down on to his chest and his body hung slack and helpless as he fought down the rising urge to pass out again.

After a few moments the feeling of sickness passed and he was able to think again. The mixture of sounds and smells that came from outside his prison made him fairly certain that he was in one of the boat slum harbours that fouled the bays and inlets around Hong Kong. He had seen them from the air just before his plane had landed and then they had been faraway and picturesque, a clogged mass of masts and sails, seething with life and festooned with drying nets. He guessed that he was on board one of the larger junks that inhabited the swarming sampan jungles.

He began to wonder why Dressler and Reutall had bothered to keep him alive, but before he could pursue the thought very far he heard a movement behind the hanging strip of matting that served as a door to his prison. The matting was suddenly pushed aside and the slim figure of Maxine Kia stepped into the cabin.

She was still wearing the silk dress of black and gold, and with her swinging ponytail of blue-black hair and her soft, delicate features she looked very young and ill-at-ease in the half light. She stared at Larren with large, dark eyes and remained with her back to the hanging matting.

"I told you that you would pay." Her voice was low and possessed a strained note of triumph. "I told you that the tong would kill you."

"I'm not dead yet," Larren said pointlessly.

"But you will die." Her voice became shriller. "You will die for the murder of my brother Cheng."

Larren winced slightly as he shifted his weight and then he said, "Just for the record I didn't kill Cheng."

"You did!" Her hand dived sharply to the broad white belt at her waist and the sharp blade of a knife glinted dully as she pulled it free. She said shrilly, "You killed Cheng with this."

Larren recognised his own sheath knife. He said flatly, "Your brother Cheng was not even killed with a knife. He was killed with one of those fancy hatchets your friends like to throw about. In fact it was probably the man called Tao Shen who killed him."

"Liar!" she cried furiously. "Tao Shen was my brother's best friend. He would never have killed Cheng."

Larren said calmly. "Why don't you go and ask him about it. I only played a small part in the affair — I ducked and allowed the hatchet to hit the wrong man."

"You lie. You lie! Dressler told me that you killed Cheng with this knife."

She raised the knife as she spoke and took an angry step forward. Larren tensed but almost immediately he relaxed again. There was something in her eyes that told him that she would not use the knife. She could stand by and order others to kill, but she was not capable of committing the act herself. She hesitated and there were tears of anger in her eyes; anger at her own weakness.

Larren gazed steadily into her eyes until at last she uttered a tiny sob and spun away. Still holding the knife she pushed her way through the door and rushed out of the cabin, her footsteps clattering up the short ladder beyond as she fled.

There was the sound of a collision as Maxine bumped into somebody on the upper deck of the junk; a brief exclamation was followed by a sob and the continued sound of her flight; then there were heavier footsteps descending the ladder. The hanging matting was again pushed aside and Dressler entered.

He regarded Larren coldly through his thick glasses, the short cane in his hand was tapping lightly against the side of his shoe.

"What have you said to Maxine?" he asked. "She seems to be upset."

Larren shrugged, a gesture that reminded him that he was still strung up in a highly uncomfortable position from the beam.

He said, "I told her that you were not really Father Christmas, and she didn't like to believe it."

Dressler smiled. "Your flippancy is pathetic. I don't know why you bother." He stepped closer and the smile vanished suddenly from his thin, bony face. He said, "Why did you come to Hong Kong, Larren?"

"To find you. Why else should I have come?"

Larren could see nothing of Dressler's eyes behind the horn-rimmed glasses and the swift cut of the cane across his ribs caught him unawares. He was unable to prevent a short yelp of agony springing up from his throat as he twisted away.

Dressler said harshly, "How did you know that Reutall and I were in Hong Kong? How did Naval Intelligence know that we were behind Maclean's kidnapping?"

Larren drew a deep breath and said, "You were careless. You should have left Maclean's kidnapping entirely to your tong friends instead of directing the operation yourself. One of the servants lived long enough to give your descriptions to the police."

Dressler scowled. "And you — how did you get involved?"

Larren saw no reason for refusing an answer and said, "Naval Intelligence circulated your descriptions around our other departments, together with a request for any known information, and as I know you both by sight I was sent out here to help."

Dressler wrinkled his face into another scowl and Larren went on. "Actually it was only Reutall's description that we were able to get, those fancy leather gloves of his make him pretty easy to recognise." He watched the sudden tenseness spring into Dressler's expression and deliberately twisted the true facts even more. "The servant who was able to talk was the old woman Reutall shot," he lied blandly. "He couldn't even aim straight. You ought to get rid of that incompetent little sadist, Dressler, he makes too many mistakes."

Dressler stared hard into Larren's face and then suddenly he laughed. "Even if Franz did make those mistakes, Larren, then they were the result of sheer bad luck and not incompetence. I have worked with him long enough to know that carelessness is not one of his faults. In fact I am more inclined to believe that you are lying in the clumsy hope of causing a quarrel between us." His teeth flashed in a quick smile. "It will not work, Larren. I am too old a hand to fall for a moth-eaten trick like that."

Larren said indifferently, "It's your funeral."

Dressler chuckled. "Wrong again, Larren, the only funeral in the near future will be yours — if they can find enough of you to bury."

He turned towards the door and then paused in the act of pushing the matting aside.

"Perhaps I shall let Franz play with you first," he said sibilantly. "He has hated you for a long time, and it would be a shame if that hate was to die without being properly released."

The door curtain swished into place behind him and he was gone.

Larren waited until the sound of footsteps had faded and then raised his face to look at the rope that secured his wrists. The rope passed over the beam above him without being knotted around it and he realised that by see-sawing his arms up and down it should be possible to chafe the rope against the beam. As the weight of his body was almost wholly supported by his arms it was excruciatingly painful to pull one arm down and raise the other, but by pressing himself up on the very tips of his toes he was able to slowly saw the rope backwards and forwards over the beam. He gritted his teeth and tried not to wonder how many hours, or even days, it would take for the rope to fray. The sweat was already running down his back and his chest and his shirt clung stickily to his body.

In a small room in a police station in Kowloon, Lieutenant-Commander Alan Kendall was listening grim-faced to a perspiring Superintendent of the Hong Kong police. The man was outlining the extent of his investigations into the murder of the Chinese businessman Cheng Kia that had taken place the previous night, and his report was not exactly encouraging.

He said, "We know that your man Larren was in the Scarlet Dragon, Commander, but we don't know what happened to him. We haven't found one witness who dares to talk. These tong killings have terrified the whole damned population. I know it sounds practically unbelievable after all these years of British rule, but the Chinese seem to be as scared as they were in the old days before the power of the tongs was smashed."

Kendall's face looked haggard beyond his years as he said wearily, "What about this tong temple you say you found when you checked the dead man's home?"

"There was nothing there that could help us. The temple was just a secret room in Cheng Kia's villa, with a lot of black drapes covering the walls and a small altar before a throne. There was a mess of dried chicken's blood on the altar but nothing more sinister than that."

"And you say there was nobody there."

"Not a soul, the whole house and the temple were empty. The only thing we could find was this." He held up two narrow strips of wrinkled silk.

Kendall took one of the strips from his hand and said slowly, "It's Larren's necktie, the one he was wearing when he left me to visit the nightclub." He looked up at the Superintendent. "This means that he must have visited Cheng's home."

The large man nodded. "The two halves of the tie were found lying on the floor of the temple, and judging by their crumpled state I should say that the tie was used to secure somebody's wrists and was later cut. But that's the only clue we have."

"I see. What do you know about this man Cheng Kia?"

"He was a pretty influential man, owning two or three large spinning mills in and around Kowloon, and until now he was always considered to be a highly respectable member of the community. That tong temple was the last thing that I would have expected to find at his home. We're doing our best to trace his friends, but a man in his position had so many acquaintances that it's hard to know where to start. We also know that there is a sister named Maxine, but she seems to have vanished. We're looking for her too."

Kendall said, "I suppose you still have no clues to the whereabouts of Commander Maclean either?"

The Superintendent spread his hands, "I'm sorry, but I haven't, We're doing everything we can but it's a very difficult job."

Kendal closed his eyes and tried to think. So far he had not only failed to find Maclean but he had lost Larren as well, and he did not know which way to turn next. The only soothing thought in the dark turmoil of his mind was the fact that all was going well with the strike party on the mainland; Paul Mason and his team were making good progress and were contacting the submarine *Watchful* every twenty-four hours to report. They had just completed their third night of marching and despite the many difficulties they had managed to cover approximately thirty-eight miles in all, and another three nights at the same pace should take them to Disaster Point. The problem was, could Maclean, and now Larren, hold out for another three days? And even if they could would they be able to give Mason's party the additional time they would need to get back to Tung Chu Bay and escape aboard the *Black Lotus*?

The doubts in his mind made Alan Kendall a very worried man.

On board the large junk where Simon Larren was held prisoner the tall man named Tao Shen was resolutely facing the sinister figure of Dressler. They were standing in a large cabin under the junk's high poop. Bright sunlight flooded down through an open skylight in the deckhead and the rough wooden furniture looked slightly more comfortable than the spartan dreariness of Larren's prison.

Tao Shen's voice was as brittle as the hard gleam in his eyes. He said, "The old arrangement is not good enough, Dressler, not any more. Cheng Kia was the overall master of the Red Hatchet Tong, and now that he is dead I take his place. If we are to continue working together then we must make a new bargain."

Dressler's thin lips parted in a brief smile as he relaxed himself comfortably in the nearest chair. Without answering he pulled a small silver hip flask from his pocket and calmly unscrewed the cap. He tilted the flask against his mouth and drank with slow contented sips. At last he lowered the flask and looked at Tao Shen.

He said, "It was a bad mistake to send you and Cheng to the Scarlet Dragon. Our informer there stressed the fact that Larren might have left at any moment, but even so it was bad judgment that allowed me to be rushed. I should have restrained my impatience and waited for another opportunity that would have enabled me to send two of your less important tong men to do the job."

Tao Shen said flatly, "The point is that Cheng Kia and I were the only two men available at such short notice, and now Cheng is dead."

"And you, as his second in command, are demanding a new deal?"

"That is so. Only this time it will be on a cash basis."

Dressler sipped more of the expensive brandy that he carried in the silver flask. His expression was hidden behind his glasses as he said:

"Cheng Kia was highly pleased with our original arrangement, and I understood that the rest of your society gave him full support."

"Cheng Kia was an idealist and a fool. He was a skilful enough politician to convince the society that his dreams would blossom, but he forgot to mention that most of us would be dead of old age before his dreams became reality. You promised that in return for our help now the leaders of

Red Hatchet Tong would be given high positions in the new Chinese government when the ninety-nine-year lease held by the British expires. But the lease still has over thirty years to go, and it will be 1997 before Hong Kong and the peninsular of the New Territories are returned to China. That time is too far off, Dressler. Cheng Kia was content to believe that one day he would have a son who would rule Hong Kong under the Communists; a son who would wield the same power of terror that Cheng's father wielded as warlord of the old Red Hatchet Tong. But I have no such dreams of future glory, and I do not trust your Communist masters to keep the promises you have made. I want my reward now."

Dressler carefully replaced the cap on his flask and returned it to his pocket. "Tao Shen," he said softly, "has it not occurred to you that the only reason I formed a partnership with Cheng Kia was to kidnap the Naval Commander Maclean. I needed men for the job and Cheng was able to supply them. Now I have Maclean, and at this very moment my good friend Franz is again trying to open his stubborn lips. Maclean cannot possibly hold out much longer, and once he talks my job here is finished. I doubt if I shall need your precious tong killers again."

Tao Shen's body stiffened with anger. "The tong has taken grave risks by coming out into the open again," he snarled angrily. "Our organisation has thrived in secret for many years, but now your demand for ritual hatchet killings to terrorise the population and lead the police away from your own motives has stirred up the British authorities again. For that and for the death of Cheng Kia who was my friend, despite his foolish ideals, you will pay now. Our services cost highly, and tong vengeance can be turned against the Communists as easily as against the British."

Dressler hissed softly, "You have made your biggest mistake, Tao Shen. I can control your tong society through Cheng Kia's sister Maxine. I do not need you. You are a dangerous man, and by threatening me you have forfeited your life."

Dressler's words gave Tao Shen a brief instant of warning, a split-second vision of what was about to come, and even as he levelled the automatic that had suddenly appeared in his hand the tall man was already springing forward. Tao Shen's face was contorted with rage and his eyes blazed with fire as he crashed into Dressler and carried both the man and the chair crashing to the floor. Simultaneously Dressler fired and the bullet slammed like the kick of a rogue elephant into Tao's body.

The Chinese man was blasted aside by the impact and rolled in a sea of fiery light and stygian darkness across the deck. Without any conscious effort he lurched to his feet, his hands were clasped to his right side where the blood was soaking through his shirt and his eyes were screwed shut. Blindly he staggered through the cabin doorway and out into the bright sunlight. He was driven by clumsy instinct that compelled him to flee and he tripped and fell helplessly over the junk's side.

He hit the surface of the water with a splash and sank down into the filthy depths. Somehow he clawed his way upwards until his head thrust out into the sunlight again, and he floundered desperately away among the closely-moored sampans.

CHAPTER 10: THE DYING TESTAMENT OF TAO SHEN

Maxine Kia stood in the bows of the large junk, her pretty nose wrinkled against the evil mixture of smells that invaded the air from the floating forest of water craft around her. Despite her distaste she could not help marvelling at the cheerful poverty of the people who lived here on the refuse-soiled waters of the boat-crammed bay, living, loving and dying beneath the pathetic canvas shelters of their sampans, the whole drama of their lives played out against the drab slum background of hanging nets and sagging lines of faded washing. From a distance there was an air of romance and excitement about the boat harbours, but from here the romance and excitement was dissolved by the rank stench of drifting garbage, and the only reality lay in the never-ending battle to simply eat, drink and live. Maxine found her thoughts vaguely troubling, and then suddenly they were banished from her mind as she heard the muffled bark of Dressler's gun.

The sound startled Maxine and she turned quickly to face the stern of the junk. Overhead a single mast supported the massive sail that was a many coloured patchwork of odd pieces of sailcloth, all sewn strongly together and stiffened by stout rods of bamboo. Below the sail a low shelter had been built amidships to protect the crew from the sun without forcing them down into the close, stuffy heat below decks; and it was this shelter that obstructed her view of the high poop and hid completely the cabin doorway where the bleeding Tao Shen stumbled out on to the deck.

It took Maxine a few moments to react to the sound of the shot and then she began to run along the port side of the junk's deck past the shelter. The thigh-length slit up one side of her dress enabled her to move swiftly but an untidy coil of rope looped across the deck caused her to stumble to her knees before she was halfway to the poop. She swore angrily as she got to her feet and found herself limping slightly from the pain of a bruised knee. By the time she reached the open deck behind the shelter Tao Shen had already vanished over the starboard side and Dressler was coming out from below the poop.

Maxine stared at the automatic in his hand and cried sharply:

"Dressler! What is happening?"

Dressler stopped dead at the sound of her cry and a twisted expression of indecision masked his face. He could hear the splashing as Tao Shen struggled away among the sampans and he had only to lean over the side to finish the man off with another shot. But if he did that then Maxine would realise the truth and that was something that he could not afford. He needed Maxine to control the sinister power of the tong, not because he foresaw any further need for more killing, but because he feared their vengeance should the true facts of the death of Cheng Kia and the shooting of Tao Shen become known.

Dressler's eyes were filled with fury behind his thick glasses and he cursed the woman silently for being so close at hand at this moment. But there was nothing he could do except lower his automatic and say harshly:

"It was nothing, Maxine. It was just a thief I caught skulking around the cabin. I took a shot at him and missed, and he dived over the side."

"A thief! Where?"

Maxine moved towards the starboard side of the junk.

Dressler jumped forward quickly and his bony hand clamped hard on her shoulder.

"Not that side," he snapped. "He went over the other side."

He turned her round forcibly and moved with her to the port side of the junk. He slipped his automatic into his pocket and waved his hand vaguely at the tightly-packed clutter of sampans.

"He's gone already," he said. "He was just some starving beggar. I was a fool to lose my head and shoot at him."

Maxine stared doubtfully at the grimy but undisturbed waters below. Her finely-arched brows were wrinkled into a frown.

She said slowly, "But I came along this side of the junk as soon as I heard your shot. I saw no one jump overboard."

Dressler's breath hissed between his teeth but he answered instantly. "It all happened very fast. The man was halfway over the ship's side before I had time to fire."

"But you were not on deck — you were only just coming out of the cabin."

Dressler said quickly, "It was in the cabin that I disturbed him. He rushed past me and knocked me down in the doorway. I pulled my revolver and fired that shot at him as he jumped over the side. I had just climbed to my feet in the cabin doorway when you came along."

The puzzled frown was still on Maxine's face as she stared at Dressler. The man's eyes were concealed behind those heavy horn-rimmed glasses and she could read nothing in his expression. He was smiling at her but his smile could have meant anything.

Then a new voice said, "I heard a shot. What is going on?"

They both turned to face the short, black-garbed figure of Franz Reutall. The little German's cherubic face was almost petulant, as though he saw some deliberate slight in the fact that guns were being fired without his knowledge.

Dressler told his story again, perfecting it as he went along. He mentally blessed his accomplice for providing him with this excuse to repeat his tale, and this time the firm confidence of his tone gave added weight to its credibility. He watched Maxine's face as he talked and felt sure that this time he had convinced her.

The tale was an obvious pack of lies to Reutall, however, for the ex S.S. man knew his comrade too well to believe that he would take such clumsy risks as firing at a stray thief.

He said suspiciously, "For a moment I thought you had probably killed Larren."

Dressler shook his head and managed to impart a brief flicker of warning to his friend, "No, Franz, you need have no fear for Larren. Now that we have been fortunate enough to capture him alive we will keep him that way for a few days; he can do us no harm where he is now, and if Maclean dies from your treatment before he talks then we will still have Larren as an alternative source of information." He smiled and added, "Once we have discovered the exact position of that sunken submarine you can enact the last rites for both of them. That is a promise."

Reutall was satisfied. He still did not know what the shooting had been about, but he guessed that Dressler would tell him as soon as Maxine was out of the way. All that was really important was that he had not been cheated out of killing Simon Larren.

He said softly, "Maclean has passed out again. I will go and revive him. Soon he will break and talk."

They watched as he turned and padded lightly away. Dressler still had his hand on Maxine's shoulder and he started to stroll calmly forwards along the deck, leading her with him and away from the poop cabin where spots of Tao Shen's blood still stained the grass matting on the floor. So far she had not thought to ask after Tao Shen, and before she did so he would have to concoct an answer that would explain the disappearance of the tall Chinese man and keep her quiet for the few days it would take for him to complete his task and leave Hong Kong.

He said casually, "This junk smells too much of fish and sweat, it is not a fit place for a young woman like you, Maxine. Is there no friend of your brother's who could hide you in some more respectable surroundings for a few days?"

Maxine shook her head. "It is a serious crime to belong to a tong, and even those among my brother's friends who are not tong men could get into trouble for hiding me. I will stay on the junk until things quieten down."

Dressler didn't answer. He was thinking that Tao Shen had been very badly wounded and that it was quite likely that the tall man had drowned in the harbour. He cursed the man for his greed and for the complications he had caused, and hoped that it was so.

From his prison below the junk's deck Simon Larren had also heard the muffled bark of Dressler's shot. He paused weakly in the painful task of sawing at the thick rope and wondered what was going on above him. His shirt was sodden with sweat now and his face was dripping in the close, suffocating heat of the tiny cabin.

He was panting hard and the agony of his arms and wrists was becoming unbearable. His head still ached and he had no idea of how long he had been struggling to free himself. The growing sense of hunger and a raging thirst told him that he had been confined for several hours, but no one had bothered to visit him since Dressler had questioned him about his mission in Hong Kong.

He strained his ears but he could hear nothing else from above, and he realised grimly that whatever was happening there was nothing he could do about it. Wearily he looked up to where his arms were stretched up to the beam above him. His wrists were already raw and there were traces of red mingling with the streams of perspiration that ran down his arms. He lifted his gaze higher to where the rope passed over the beam and saw that it was at last showing slight signs of fraying.

With savage determination he pushed himself up again on the tips of his toes and renewed the agonising see-sawing of his arms that chafed the rope against the beam. His muscles burned in protest and it seemed as though his arms must be dragged out of their sockets as he worked. His grey-green eyes — eyes that some men had aptly described as the eyes of a killer — glowered painfully and angrily in his lean face.

Maxine was leaning against the junk's mast just forward of the rude shelter that graced the vessel's deck. Above her the spread sail was shadowing her from the direct heat of the sun. The sounds of the sampan jungle still throbbed around her, unperturbed by the brief bark of the gun that had been fired less than thirty minutes ago. The sound had been slightly muffled by the cabin walls, and those who knew enough to recognise the sound for what it was had blandly ignored it. The life around the junk had to go on. A sound that might have been a gunshot was nobody's business, and it was best to leave it that way.

Dressler had finally left her alone and Maxine was glad, for she did not particularly like or trust the man. She had taken a dislike to both Dressler and Reutall from the moment that her brother Cheng had first introduced her, and now that their presence had indirectly caused her brother's death her dislike deepened. She found herself hoping that Kolo, who was now ashore buying stores and vegetables, would soon return. The Mongol giant was the only friend she really trusted now that Cheng was dead, he had been her devoted servant since childhood and she knew that he would obey her every command without any hesitation. Kolo was her only rock in a sea of intrigue, for even Tao Shen was too ambitious to be trusted now.

The memory of Tao Shen sent an uneasy ripple across the surface of her thoughts. She suddenly realised that she had not seen the tall man who had taken her brother's place since before Dressler shot at the thief in the poop cabin. It was strange that he had not been attracted on deck by the sound of the shot.

She felt her original doubts returning again and moved thoughtfully to the junk's side to stare down into the water. There was nothing to be seen now except a mess of peelings and a few tins and rags floating past on the oily surface. She found herself wondering whether Dressler had been telling her the truth and wished again that Kolo would return.

She was about to turn away when a small, flat-bottomed boat nosed its way slowly out from among the lanes of sampans. In the stern a ragged young Chinese boy of eleven or twelve years of age was leaning his thin body against the long steering pole as he guided the clumsy craft towards the junk. He was wearing a large straw coolie hat that hid almost the whole of his face, and his splayed legs were bare-footed as he stood in the bottom of his boat. He had to crane his head back a long way to see up from under his hat, and when he saw Maxine he allowed the square nose of his boat to bump against the junk's hull directly below her.

He said nervously, "You missy Maxine Kia? Yes? Yes?"

Maxine could only nod her head in surprise.

"You come. You come with me. Man ask for you." His voice was quick and strained. "You come now."

Maxine found her voice. "What man?" she demanded. "What are you talking about?"

"Man in water. Chinese man. Very sick." One skinny arm waved expressively. "Man sick. Much blood. Man say — go to big junk, ask for Maxine Kia. Nobody else. Just bring Maxine Kia."

Quite suddenly Maxine knew that he was talking about Tao Shen. Tao's failure to appear after the shot and Dressler's clumsy explanation about a mysterious thief fitted neatly together now. The sick man the boy spoke of could only be Tao Shen.

Maxine looked swiftly around the deserted deck of the junk and then back at the boy. "All right. I'm coming," she said. And without hesitation she swung her slim body over the junk's side and dropped lightly into the frail boat beneath. The boat rocked wildly and she fell to her knees, clutching at each of the shallow sides with her hands.

"Quickly," she ordered. "Take me to this sick Chinese man."

The boy needed no urging for he was obviously frightened of remaining near the junk, and with a thankful nod he poled swiftly away. A few seconds later they were safely hidden between the rows of floating sampans.

Here the foul smells that filled the air were even stronger, and Maxine made a futile effort at holding her breath. Dirty but grinning children stared at them from the passing sampans, and chickens and other livestock cackled or yelped as they slid by, and Maxine wondered how they all managed to survive against such a background. The straining boy wielded his pole to guide them through the maze and seemed totally unaffected by the sounds and smells. Instead he was casting nervous glances along the disturbed stretch of soiled water in their wake.

Not more than fifty yards away, and still in clear view of the large sail of the junk, the boy dug his pole deep to stop the boat's drifting progress. The boat swung level with a moored sampan and Maxine was aware of an old man in filthy clothes who was reaching out to pull the boat closer. His gnarled fingers closed over the boat's side, and Maxine straightened up to look into the sampan. A canvas shelter stretched over hoops of bamboo covered the centre of the sampan, and the hanging nets that draped over everything told that the old man was a fisherman. In the canvas shelter lay the still form of Tao Shen, his clothing was sodden and the plank bottom of the sampan was covered with pools of water where his body lay. The whole region of his right side was red with blood and his breathing was a frightening, rattling sound in his throat.

The old fisherman was as nervous as his son as he helped Maxine into the sampan.

"We find him in the water," he said in a cracked and wheezy voice that was almost a whine. "He ask for Missy Maxine Kia. I do not think he will live."

Maxine felt as though the very air was strangling her and there was a horribly twisted feeling in her stomach. She ignored the old man and moved closer to Tao Shen. The dying man's eyes were wide open and he was staring up at her. She tried to say something but her mouth had dried up.

Tao said weakly, "Listen, Maxine. I have to warn you. Dressler is not to be trusted. It was he who shot me when I asked for a new deal. He thinks — he thinks he can control Red Hatchet Tong through you. He said he did not need me."

Tao's eyes were fixed on her face and he was pressing his hand against the wound in his side. The dark red life's blood was squeezing out slowly through his fingers.

"Beware of him, Maxine. Cheng Kia and I made a great mistake in believing his promises. Do not allow him to fool you too."

A fit of coughing stopped Tao Shen's voice and his body writhed in pain. Maxine suddenly found the will to move and she dropped on to her knees by his side. Gently she lifted his shoulders on to her lap, cradling his head with her arm.

"Tao," she said desperately. "Tao, you must not die. You must not. I need you."

Tao Shen rallied the last of his strength and said:

"There is something else, Maxine. I must confess it. It was I who struck the blow that killed your brother Cheng — not the man Larren. Cheng was to delay Larren and hold him in the darkness while I killed him from behind, but Larren ducked and the hatchet killed my best friend." He choked again and his words became even more forced than before. "Don't go back to the junk, Maxine. It is too dangerous. If Dressler realises that you know the truth he will kill you too."

A spasm of pain made his body jerk and Maxine held him tightly against her. "Tao," she cried. "Tao, please…"

Tao Shen opened his eyes for the last time. "Don't go back to the junk," he said faintly, and then slowly his eyes glazed over.

Maxine stared down at the dead man in her arms, and for a moment she was just a tiny, frightened woman, her eyes clouded by the shock of death. Then her face hardened and she became the daughter of a tong warlord and the sister of a tong killer. She ran grim hands through Tao Shen's clothing and uttered a short exclamation of satisfaction as she found what she wanted.

She stood up with Tao Shen's automatic in her hand and said firmly:

"Take me back to the junk."

The old fisherman looked down at the corpse.

"But what about him? What must I do?"

Maxine said bitterly, "He is dead, he can feel nothing — what does it matter."

She stepped back into the small boat where the old man's son still waited.

"Take me back," she said harshly. "I wish to go back to the junk."

The boy glanced at his father, but he saw nothing but fear in the old man's eyes. Resignedly he began to pole the frail boat back towards the large junk.

The old fisherman wrung his hands and stared helplessly at Maxine's retreating back, but the woman did not look round. The stark fear that had gripped her while Tao Shen lay dying in her arms had receded before the cold anger that now lay like an icy shroud around her heart. The automatic in her hand was warm from close contact with Tao's body, and she found herself wishing that it was a red hatchet instead. Dressler deserved to die by tong vengeance, but at least he would die.

The boat was bumping against the junk again and Maxine scrambled without hesitation to the ship's deck. The terrified fisherboy immediately began to pole his craft back into the sampans but Maxine did not wait to watch him go. She moved swiftly along the deck towards the poop. The upper decks of the junk were deserted and she reached the doorway to the poop cabin unseen. Here she paused and listened until she heard the sounds of a man moving inside. Her lips tightened and her hand grew white around the gun as she pushed the door open and stepped inside.

Dressler turned round to face her as she entered. He was alone, and his body froze at the sight of the automatic.

He said tensely, "Maxine! What is the meaning of this?"

Her voice was cold. "It means that I have been talking to Tao Shen. And it means that you are going to die."

Dressler licked his lips. "So Tao Shen is still alive."

"He is dead now, murdered by you. But before he died he sent for me and told me the truth."

"The truth?" Dressler forced a laugh. "I doubt very much whether Tao Shen told you the truth my dear Maxine. He probably told a very good story — but not the truth."

Maxine said viciously. "Save your breath, Dressler. I did not come here to listen to more of your lies." She raised the automatic and finished softly, "I came to kill you."

Another second and Dressler would have died, but Maxine was not granted that single second. A black-gloved hand closed on the long ponytail of her hair and wrenched her head back and downwards, bending her body in a savage, backward arch that made her scream with pain. In the same moment a second black-gloved hand seized her wrist and twisted the automatic from her fingers.

Franz Reutall continued to hold her in that cruel, merciless grip as he said softly, "Now you must die, Miss Maxine. What a great, great shame."

Deep in the gloomy tomb of the junk's hull Simon Larren fell crashing to the deck as the rope that had held him up finally broke under his weight. He lay in a half-conscious daze of pain and sweat and the smell of blood from his bleeding wrists. Then slowly, very slowly, he began to stir.

CHAPTER 11: MAXINE DISAPPEARS

The silky tone of Reutall's voice seemed to drain the strength from Maxine's body. She fell back against him and was forced to her knees by that agonising pull at her hair. The fear that had gripped her while she held the dying Tao Shen came swirling back to engulf her like the dark rush of a cold night wind. Her head was still held back and she found herself looking up into the face of the man behind her; Reutall's chubby face was beaming but his eyes were mere slits of gleaming sadism in the flesh of his face. He had released her wrist now that she had dropped the automatic and the cold wind froze in her stomach as his leather-clad hand stroked the taut line of her white throat.

"A great shame," he repeated. "Such a great, great shame." Maxine almost screamed again at the revolting touch of that evil, black hand, and her arched body twisted desperately as she fought to free herself. Reutall held her easily, his grip almost tearing the long ponytail of her hair from her head, and at last she became still, her eyes full of tears and terror.

Dressler came slowly forward to pick up the gun that she had dropped and then regarded her balefully. Maxine's position made him look much taller than he really was as he stood over her and he fingered the automatic thoughtfully. When he spoke his voice was smooth and without emotion.

"As Franz says, Maxine, it is a great shame. I had such high hopes that you and I could work together, but now it seems that I must kill you too."

Maxine could not answer him and he went on.

"Of course I do not blame you. I blame Tao Shen, and my own indiscretion in killing him, or rather attempting to, while you were still aboard this junk." He paused. "By the way, where did you see Tao Shen?"

Maxine stared at him without answering until Reutall wrenched gently at her hair. Then her throat worked helplessly before she said:

"He was lying in a sampan. An old fisherman took him aboard."

"So he did not drown — a pity. It means that we must now vacate this junk. A dead body will not be overlooked in the same manner as a stray shot."

Maxine found a little of her former anger and said:

"The tong will make you pay for this. We have protected you from the authorities — but there is nothing that can protect you from the tong."

Dressler sighed. "I will admit that the thought has occurred to me, but it is a chance that I must take. If I allowed you to live now I would still have trouble with your tong friends for killing Tao Shen, so really I have nothing to lose."

He looked down at the automatic in his hand and then carefully put the weapon into his jacket pocket. He turned and walked over to the table at the far end of the cabin. As he came back he said quietly:

"I think this will serve our purpose better than a gun. It belonged to Tao Shen but he was forced to leave it behind."

The cold wind of terror swirled anew through Maxine's body and she uttered a choking scream that was strangled at birth by Reutall's crushing fingers on her throat.

The weapon that Dressler held was a short tong hatchet, both the handle and the blade of which had been painted a bright blood red.

Below the junk's deck Simon Larren was on his hands and knees. He struggled upright and lurched over to the bulkhead, propping himself up while he gulped in deep mouthfuls of the stale air. Grimly he began to move his aching arms, flexing his shoulder muscles to take away the stiffness. The two halves of the broken rope dangled from his raw wrists like dancing snakes as he worked. His head still ached badly and on touching it he found a sticky mess of dried blood where Dressler's blow had broken the skin. The thought of Dressler sent a cold, silent fury surging through his frame that slowly began to take control of his congealed lips.

He remembered the shot he had heard and wondered whether it had spelt the end of the gallant Maclean; perhaps the navy man had talked at last and so put his usefulness to an end. He decided that the only way to find out was to get a move on and take a look around. If Maclean was still alive he would try to take him with him; if not he would have to escape to warn Kendall, and the strike party on the mainland.

He pushed himself away from the wall and stood for a moment in the centre of the cabin. Now that the initial weariness had worn off he found that he was quite steady despite the abominable ache of his arms and the throbbing of his head. Twenty-four hours sleep and a honey blonde to massage his hurts and he would be fit again, he told himself grimly. Meanwhile he would have to make an attempt to find Maclean as he was.

He pushed aside the hanging matting that formed the door of his cabin and found himself facing a rickety wooden ladder that led up to the deck. Behind the ladder was a large hold that smelt even more strongly of fish. Larren peered into the gloom and satisfied himself that the hold was empty before starting up the ladder. Halfway up he felt suddenly dizzy and almost slipped back into the hold, then slowly the attack passed and he began to climb again.

He stopped once his eyes reached deck level and felt a fresh wave of throbbing spread through his skull as he twisted his head around to make sure that the deck was deserted. There was no one else on deck and he hauled himself out of the hatchway, feeling a sudden sense of relief now that he was no longer in danger of tumbling off the ladder.

He was standing just forward of the mast and the shelter that had been built amidships and he moved into the shadows by the rough wall of the shelter as he breathed deeply at the sunlit air. It still tasted of fish and sweat but it was pure fragrance after the stench below. He turned at last to continue his search and almost fell over the wooden bucket that stood on the junk's deck. The bucket was full of brackish water that both looked and smelt vile. Larren stared at it for a moment and then he lifted it up and poured the cool water gratefully over his face, chest and shoulders. The soaking refreshed him and helped to clear the last haze of fog from his brain. He replaced the bucket and drew a deep breath before moving stealthily aft along the junk's deck.

He took a brief look inside the shelter but found it empty except for a few more pieces of crude wooden furniture and an open cupboard containing a few chipped rice bowls and other pieces of crockery. It seemed that this was just the crew's eating quarters and Larren turned to move on. Then he noticed that one of the clumsy wooden chairs was almost falling apart, and was sagging badly where one splayed leg was almost out of its socket. He picked the chair up and with one wrench he tore the chair leg free. He gripped it like a club and felt slightly more confident as he left the shelter.

He crossed the short stretch of open deck between the shelter and the poop and hesitated near the poop cabin door. There was another hatch in the centre of that square of deck and he wondered whether Maclean might be down there. Then he suddenly heard Dressler's voice from inside the cabin.

He pressed up against the bulkhead, his eyes were hard and his knuckles were glaring white where he gripped his improvised club. He found a tiny chink in the rough planking and peered into the gloom of the cabin. He saw Maxine held fast in Reutall's sadistic hands; and Dressler standing over her with the tong hatchet.

Dressler was saying:

"Another tong killing will keep the inhabitants of these stinking sampans quiet, and the use of Tao Shen's hatchet will help to confuse your murderous friends."

Larren clenched his teeth as he wrestled with a sudden rush of indecision. His job was to find Maclean, not to worry about the fate of a woman who had once screamed for his blood; and whichever one he chose to save he would lose all opportunity of helping the other. He told himself savagely that Maxine Kia deserved nothing better than death, and deliberately he turned away. His job was to find Maclean, and there would never be a better time than now, while Dressler and Reutall busied themselves with Maxine.

Then Maxine uttered a single shriek of terror, and the sound brought a grim memory rushing back with startling clarity to his mind. He saw his wife, Andrea, the only woman he had ever loved, the woman he had worshipped with body, heart and soul; his beautiful Andrea who had died beneath a shattering burst of gunfire in a Paris back street as the result of direct orders from the spy ring of whom Dressler and Reutall were now the only surviving members. Andrea too had shrieked as she died, and Larren saw her fall again as Maxine's cry speared through his brain.

Nothing could have stopped Larren then; not a thousand gallant men or a million sunken submarines. Vengeance and hatred flamed in twin bursts of fire from a white hot core deep inside him, and like a man possessed he crashed bodily into the cabin.

Dressler was in the very act of raising the hatchet and the scream was still in Maxine's throat as she fought to twist away. Dressler let out an angry yell and then Larren whirled his crude club in a smashing blow that sent the thin man sprawling. His free hand closed on Maxine's arm and he yanked her to her feet, tearing her from the startled Reutall's grasp. Larren kicked out savagely with his foot, booting the black-gloved sadist squarely on the spot where his enemies had operated on him so long ago. Reutall screeched hideously and fell reeling back against the wall.

Larren swung his club back again, tensing for a blow that would have crushed the German's skull into a grey and bloody pulp. Then Maxine screamed a warning and he turned to see Dressler wrenching an automatic from his pocket as he struggled up from the deck. Larren hurled his club as the man fired and both of them missed in their haste.

The bark of the gun and the sound of Maxine's voice brought sanity back to Larren's brain. Maxine was staring up at him and she was not his beloved Andrea. Dressler had slipped back to the floor but was already bringing his gun up for another shot.

As the burst of madness died Larren knew that Dressler would not miss a second time, and the man was too far away for him to leap on to the skinny frame. Savagely Larren sprang for the door, dragging Maxine with him as he burst out on to the deck. He was only just in time for the second shot from Dressler's gun tore through the opening behind him and only just missed as he twisted away.

Maxine was running beside him, her wrist still clamped fast in his hand as they sprinted along the deck. Larren pulled her to a stop in the junk's bows, directly opposite the nearest moored sampan.

"Jump!" he ordered harshly, and together they leaped over the junk's side. They cleared the intervening stretch of dirty water and landed with a crash in the bottom of the sampan. The craft rocked wildly and Maxine yelped with pain as she cracked her shin and fell forwards. Larren heard the angry yelling of Dressler's voice and looked back to see the man racing after them along the junk's deck.

He turned back to Maxine and heaved her to her feet. She sobbed for breath and stumbled after him as he ducked low through the canvas shelter that was stretched over the centre of the sampan. They reached the stern of the craft and then jumped for the next one that was only a few feet away. An old Chinese woman screamed and her man yelled angrily as they pushed past them and blundered down the centre of the sampan, ducking again beneath the canvas shelter.

There was an uproar of further shouts and screams as Larren dragged the stumbling woman through half a dozen sampans in quick succession. Chickens squawked under their feet and children began to howl as they passed. One furious owner made a clumsy attempt to stop them but Larren sent the man flying into the harbour with a vicious swing of his fist. Then, as they jumped for yet another sampan, Larren slipped; he missed his footing and plunged into the stinking water, still dragging Maxine down with him.

He had to release Maxine as the water closed over his head and he clawed his way frantically to the surface. His head burst out into the sunlight again and he spat out a mouthful of filthy water as he swam back to the sampan. Maxine was already on the surface and pulling herself over the sampan's low side and she turned to help him in. Her gorgeous dress of black and gold silk was sodden and clinging wetly to the high curve of her breasts, and the natural slit at the thigh had torn even higher to reveal the smooth white flesh above her stocking as she knelt to pull him into the boat.

Larren fell on to the deck of the sampan beside her, his chest heaving as he retched up more of the foul water he had swallowed. Now that the continued progress of his flight had been stopped the reaction that stemmed from his original hurts began to soak through him. His brain was reeling under the battery of pain waves that radiated from the back of his head and for the moment he could do nothing but sprawl helplessly and retch.

Maxine looked up into the face of the elderly Chinaman whose sampan they had invaded. The man was cowering back beneath the canvas hood in the middle of the boat, his eyes were wild and frightened and he was holding tightly to an equally terrified woman who was obviously his wife.

Maxine said quickly, "Do not be afraid. We will not hurt you. But you must find a boat to take us to the shore." The old man merely cowered back deeper below the hood and she cried desperately, "I will pay you well — anything you ask."

Slowly the old man raised his arm and pointed to the stern of the sampan.

"There is a boat," he quavered. "Take it — but leave us in peace."

Maxine glanced round fearfully. The people in the adjoining sampans were shouting and staring but were making no physical attempt to interfere. She could still see the high sail of the junk above the sampans, but there was no sign of any pursuit from Dressler. Larren still lay helpless before her, his last burst of strength completely spent.

Quickly Maxine got to her feet and scrambled through the hood shelter past the old man and his wife. She almost entangled herself in a curtain of hanging nets in her haste as she came out in the stern of the boat. Frantically she wriggled free and saw a small flat-bottomed boat moored to the sampan. She jumped swiftly aboard and untied the rope, then pulled herself hand over hand along the side of the sampan until she was opposite Larren.

Despite her entreaties the old man was too frightened to help her to get the Englishman into the boat, but Larren found another small reserve of strength to help himself and caused the smaller boat to rock dangerously as he literally fell aboard. Maxine threw a handful of Hong Kong dollars on to the deck of the sampan and said:

"We will leave the boat at the quay. You can send a friend to pick it up."

The old man stared but made no answer and Maxine dug the steering pole that had laid in the boat deep into the water and began to pole away. Larren lay stretched out between her feet, gazing up at the tense lines of her body beneath her dripping dress. He decided that she could pole just as well as he would be able to and thankfully closed his eyes. His head was aching with concentrated fury and he felt more dead than alive.

Maxine steered a zig-zag course through the jungle of sampans, just in case Dressler was trying to follow them. The tiny boat lay low in the water due to Larren's weight, but it moved swiftly enough as she thrust hard at the pole. She worked strenuously for ten minutes and then the harbour wall appeared out of the mass of water craft and she turned towards it.

"Wake up, Larren," she said urgently as their boat bumped against the quayside. "Wake up, please."

The desperation in her voice roused Larren out of his stupor of pain and weariness and with an effort he struggled halfway to his feet. She helped him with insistent hands and pushed him up onto the quay. Larren swayed unsteadily until she climbed up beside him and by then his brain was beginning to function again.

"Telephone," he said grimly. "I must find a telephone."

"This way." She guided him past gaping coolies and fishermen mending their nets; past playing children who stopped their games to stare, and through a maze of coiled ropes and suspended nets that were hanging out to dry.

Larren trusted her blindly, his eyes half closed against the pain in his head. His only thought now was to find a telephone; to report to Alan Kendall and pray that the Naval man could lay on a raid to the junk fast enough to help Maclean.

Maxine led him into the foyer of the first building they came to — a cheap hotel — and Larren almost collapsed against the desk where a Chinese clerk was dozing sleepily. His hand was already on the desk telephone and he had half dialled his number before the man knew what was happening.

The clerk yelled angrily and Larren turned and snarled at him to keep quiet. The man backed up nervously and did not attempt to protest again.

Larren burned with impatience until he heard the polite voice of a secretary at Naval Headquarters. He snapped into the mouthpiece and moments later he heard the welcome sound of Alan Kendall anxiously asking what the hell was going on.

Larren told him as briefly as he could; pausing only once to ask Maxine the name of the junk and of the harbour.

Kendall said grimly, "I'll have a swarm of police down there as fast as possible. Where are you speaking from now?"

Larren looked round at Maxine but she had been standing close enough to hear the question and was already demanding the information from the scowling clerk.

The man said, "This is Wing Soo's hotel."

Larren passed the fact on to Kendall who rapped back. "Stay there, Larren. I'm on my way."

The phone clicked as Kendall rang off and Larren wearily replaced his receiver on its rest.

He said slowly, "If this is a hotel then you'll have rooms. We'll take one for the rest of the day."

"No rooms," said the clerk sourly.

Maxine slapped a fistful of notes on the desk.

"One room," she said curtly. "A good one." And it was the voice of a tong warlord's daughter that spoke.

The clerk hesitated, but there was something in Maxine's tone that was backed up by the glare in Larren's eyes. He picked up the notes and slowly handed them a key.

"Room twenty-seven," he muttered surlily. "First floor."

Maxine took the key without another word and helped to support Larren as they crossed the foyer to the staircase that led to the upper rooms. Somewhat unsteadily they moved up the stairs to the landing. Maxine hesitated for a moment and then turned left along a musty corridor. Three doors down she found number twenty-seven and let herself in with the key.

The room was cheaply furnished with a washstand, a chest of drawers and a sagging double bed. Maxine kicked the door shut behind her and helped Larren to the bed. Larren fell back gratefully.

She looked down at him and said softly:

"Sleep, my brave friend, there is nothing you can do now until your comrades come to find you." Her hand rested gently on his sweating forehead and she added: "You are safe enough with me."

Larren was already unconscious; now that the danger was gone he had finally succumbed to the stealing blackness that had crept over his senses. Maxine sat on the bed beside him and carefully began to pick at the knotted ropes that still hung from his bleeding wrists.

The sound of Alan Kendall's voice and the liquid fire of whisky burning his lips were the first sensations that came to Larren's brain when he recovered. He choked and slowly opened his eyes.

Kendall was standing over him, supporting him with one arm and holding a glass to his lips. There were two other men in the room whom Larren did not know, and at first everything was strange and he wondered where he was. Then memory returned as he looked around the drab room with its paint-peeling walls, and he remembered Maxine Kia bringing him here after he had phoned Kendall.

He said weakly, "Maclean — did you find him?"

Kendall said slowly, "I'm sorry, Larren. I did my best but when we raided the junk it was empty. There wasn't a soul aboard her."

Larren was silent, bitterness and anger mingling within him as he realised that despite everything that had happened since he had first entered the Scarlet Dragon they were still back where they had started: Maclean was still missing.

Kendall went on, "You've had a tough time, Larren, but I had to drag you back to the world of the living. Is there anything you can tell me that will give us a lead to where Dressler might have gone now? Anything at all?"

Larren said, "Ask Maxine. She might know."

Kendall said grimly, "If you mean the woman who brought you here that's impossible. She disappeared completely before we arrived. The clerk below says he doesn't know where she went."

CHAPTER 12: INVITATION TO LOVE

The first grey chinks of dawn were beginning to crack through the fading blackness of night but it was still bitterly cold. Five men were toiling up the steep slope of a rugged range of hills towards a dense cluster of pines where they intended to rest and conceal themselves throughout the coming day. Each man was bent low, as much by the killing weight of his pack as by the need to remain hidden. They were breathing heavily and every muscle of their bodies ached with the steady, gnawing weariness that had grown upon them with every hour of the long, tiring night.

They reached the miniature forest and Paul Mason led them cautiously among the slim boles of the trees. There was vegetation here, low, coarse bracken that would be just tall enough to hide them provided they lay flat, and it was here that Mason stopped. He turned towards them and said quietly:

"This will have to do, it's nearly daylight. Wait here for me while I find out how far these trees extend."

The remaining four men nodded silently and gratefully lowered their packs from their bowed shoulders. Mason left his own pack behind and continued alone into the gloomy darkness between the pines. He knew he should be sending one of the two Chinese guides — it was their job to scout for the simple reason that they were the only two who could bluff their way out of any trouble they might encounter — but he knew that Fen Liu and Chao Lin were both much more tired than he was. They were good men, but neither of them had the stamina to stand any more marching tonight.

Mason himself was feeling the strain of four nights' marching, but he knew that somebody had to scout around and make sure that there were no farmhouses or similar habitations nearby. He reached the far edge of the small forest where the grey streaks of dawn were penetrating more deeply through the branches and moved more cautiously.

Beyond the edge of the trees there was a gentle slope that rose to the crest of the ridge that they had been climbing. Mason stooped low as he climbed those last few yards and keenly surveyed the valley beyond. There was a dim vista of flat paddy-fields sweeping away in the faint morning light. A low mist lay along the centre of the valley and a few crude stone farmhouses rose above it like clumsy ships becalmed on a white sea. A dog barked somewhere below but both the sound and the buildings were too far off to cause any threat.

Mason backed away and retreated into the thick shadows below the trees. Dry twigs crackled under his feet as he searched for his companions and eventually he heard the soft Scottish burr of Hugh Logan's voice guiding him home.

Logan was on his feet waiting for him; the two guides were sprawling exhausted on a carpet of wet moss and bracken; Randell, the second Sergeant, was carefully fixing up their radio. Mason looked at the luminous face of his watch and saw that it was time he made his daily call to the submarine *Watchful* that still lurked out at sea.

Logan said quietly, "We did well today, Captain. Another two nights at this pace should bring us to Disaster Point."

Mason nodded and said, "I shall be damned glad to get there. Once we've done the job we can at least dump these blasted aqualung outfits. After this the return hike will be a picnic."

They both relapsed into silence as Randell began calling the listening submarine. There was no sound now in the dark glade except the insistent sound of Randell's low voice and the slight crackle of the radio.

Mason scowled as he listened. Randell was having trouble again and the radio was acting as though it was about to pack up. They had had difficulty in contacting *Watchful* the previous evening and now it looked as though the failure of the set was going to be their first setback.

Then at last Randell said, "I've contacted *Watchful*, sir. The signal's weak but they're coming through."

Mason's scowl faded and he thought that at least they were going to get through tonight, even if it was for the last time. He took Randell's place before the small radio transmitter and quietly and briefly gave his report.

A few hours after Mason's report had been sent by coded signal from *Watchful* to Hong Kong, Simon Larren was listening to a verbal version of it from Alan Kendall.

They were seated in Larren's hotel room in Victoria, not the cheap room that Maxine Kia had taken him to but the room that had been booked for him before he flew into Hong Kong. Kendall had driven him there after Maxine's disappearance, and now, after fourteen hours' of rest and a liberal dosing of medicinal whisky, he was back on his feet again. The back of his head was still sore beneath the large piece of plaster that a Naval doctor had applied and his wrists were neatly bandaged, but he insisted that he was fit enough to work.

He listened to what Kendall had to say and then took another sip at his neat medicine before replying.

"So Mason and his party are still penetrating behind the enemy lines. They're doing well and it's a pity that we're letting them down at this end."

Kendall said grimly, "I'm doing everything possible. I've got my own department concentrating on nothing but Maclean's kidnapping, and I've got practically the whole of Hong Kong's police force on it as well. But everybody concerned seems to have completely disappeared. We can't even find your Maxine Kia, and according to you she's shifted over to our side."

Larren said quietly, "I can understand Maxine doing the vanishing act, she was mixed up too deeply with this tong affair."

"Maybe, but it doesn't help us to find Maclean. We seem to have run right out of leads."

Larren said thoughtfully, "There is still one lead."

"What's that?"

"The first one we had: the Scarlet Dragon and Nancy Kang." He looked sharply at Kendall. "She hasn't done a vanishing trick too, has she?"

"No. But I don't see how that's going to help, as she knows you. And besides, look what happened last time."

Larren said slowly, "I'm not really sure whether Nancy did send for Dressler or not. Dressler said that I had been recognised at the airport and hinted that I had been watched ever since. And anyway, even if he did receive word from somebody at the club, it doesn't necessarily have to be Nancy."

Kendall said doubtfully, "Either way, she still knows that you're on our side."

Larren shrugged. "You're my boss, Commander, but if you have no alternative orders then there's no reason why I shouldn't have another talk to Nancy Kang. Even if I do draw a blank it won't have cost us anything."

Kendall said, "All right, Larren, you can give it a try. But for God's sake don't go A.W.O.L. again."

Larren grinned. "This time I'm going in daylight, then nobody can switch off the lights."

The Wan Chai district of Kowloon looked almost as sleazy in the hot afternoon sunlight as it did at night when it was ablaze with neon. Larren walked slowly down a crowded street where children played on the pavements and a swarming throng of faces swirled by. His gaze searched among the gaudy Chinese banners above the heads of the crowd for the sign of the Scarlet Dragon.

It took him some time to find the place and when he did so he could have sworn that it had been moved from its previous position; the densely-packed streets were so similar that it was hard to tell one from another. He pushed his shoulder through an intervening mass of people and stepped through the open door.

The place was in half darkness, and apart for one solitary customer and the waiter behind the bar it was empty. Larren noted that the barman was not the same man who had been on duty the night that Cheng Kia had died and wondered whether the man had quit. He shrugged the thought aside and crossed over to the bar.

The barman said politely, "I am sorry, sir. We are not open."

Larren glanced at the single customer but decided not to protest. Instead he said:

"I'm looking for Miss Nancy Kang. Is she available?"

The barman hesitated for a moment and then a calm voice from behind Larren's back said softly:

"She is."

Larren turned to face the stage. It had been empty when he came in but now Nancy Kang was standing there and regarding him with a slow smile. She wore the same red dress that he had seen her in before, and she was deliberately standing so that the long slit up one side fell away from the smooth line of her leg and thigh.

Larren strolled casually towards her.

"I came to apologise," he said simply. "The last time that I was here I had to rush out without saying goodbye."

He stopped in front of her and she looked down at him from the raised dais of the stage. Her eyes were shining with a strange light beneath her slanting eyebrows, but her mouth moulded softly into a sudden smile.

"And now you have apologised?"

Larren smiled back at her. "I'm a television scout, remember — and you promised to demonstrate some of your talents."

Nancy Kang laughed and stepped down beside him.

"You are a strange man," she said, "and an intriguing one. I ought to slap your handsome face and send you away, but there is something about you that attracts me."

Larren raised his eyebrows. "The effect is mutual."

"You laugh at me — but it does not matter." Her smile broadened. "I think perhaps that the women you have known do not usually admit it when they find a man attractive. But I am like no woman you have ever known. I live   and love — by rules of my own making, not by those of society." Her thigh brushed lingeringly against his own as she turned away and she finished softly. "Come, follow me." She glanced over her shoulder as she spoke and again there was that strange gleam beneath her slanting brows.

Larren was still wary, but he followed her. She led him through the hanging curtains behind the stage and down a short corridor that brought them out on to the street. Taking his arm she turned left and guided him along the crowded pavement.

"Where are we going?" he asked calmly.

"To my apartment, it is only a few yards down the street." Her smile mocked him. "Does that not please you?"

Larren smiled and shrugged, he wasn't really sure whether it pleased him or not, he still hadn't decided what game she was playing.

They were silent after that as they weaved a path through the mass of people jamming the pavement. Then Nancy turned him into a narrow street that was colourful with cheap awnings overhanging the pavement; jumbles of baskets and wares obstructed every doorway and long shop signs hung every few yards along the road. There was a clinging host of smells; sweet, rancid, sickly, the smell of spices, of garlic and of ripe fruit. Above all there was the noisy blare of loudly-tuned radios and the shrill cries of vendors shouting their wares.

Nancy stopped at last before a narrow doorway between two of the shops. She led him inside and up a steep flight of stairs. At the top of the landing she turned right and produced a key to unlock the nearest door. She invited him inside and he crossed the threshold with his mind and body alert for any surprise attack, but the room was empty and she shut the door behind him.

The room was surprisingly clean compared to the sleazy street outside. It was a living-room, sparsely furnished with a low table and some modern-styled chairs, coloured mats on the floor and bright watercolours on the wall gave it a pleasing appearance.

Nancy turned to face Larren and said coyly, "You like it? I am glad. Here we can talk, and you can tell me why you really came to see me."

She tried to sound naive as she spoke, but her smile gave her away. Larren rested his hands on her shoulders and for a moment she pressed her lithe body against him. Her eyes were looking up into his and this time the gleam in their dark depths was one of clear invitation. Her lips were red and shining, raised for his kiss, but when he attempted to respond she jerked her head back and ducked swiftly away.

She stood back a pace and chuckled. "Now I know why you came."

Larren shrugged. "All right, I'll confess. I'm a lipstick salesman. I was merely about to show you what an inferior quality you're wearing before I start my sales talk."

Nancy laughed. "You are a rogue and a lecher — nothing more, nothing less." She glanced down suddenly to where the high split of her dress was revealing the round curve of her thigh. "I think I will change this dress," she remarked. "It is all right for singing in a nightclub, but to entertain a man — no, it makes him think that I am a bad woman."

She moved lightly over to the far side of the room and opened the door that obviously led to her bedroom. She leaned in the doorway for a moment and said, "There is drink in the small cupboard, help yourself and pour one for me. I shall not be long."

The door closed behind her and Larren stared at it thoughtfully. Then he moved over to the cupboard she had indicated and opened it to inspect the selection of bottles. He still couldn't make up his mind whether Nancy Kang was baiting a trap for him or not.

Giving up the problem for the moment he poured himself a whisky. He drank it slowly and appreciatively and then called out to ask Nancy what she was drinking. When she answered he poured out two more whiskies and carried them to the bedroom door. There he waited, suddenly sure of what was going to happen next.

Nancy Kang called huskily, "Bring mine in here, darling."

Larren's mouth hardened and he was certain that there would be somebody waiting behind that door. That was why she had brought him here. He drained one glass at a single swallow, then he set the glass down and lightly gripped the door handle. He thrust the door open and moved swiftly into the room, his body tensed to throw the neat spirit in his hand straight into the eyes of whoever was waiting.

There was nobody there.

Larren stopped awkwardly just inside the bedroom. Like the living-room it was cheaply but attractively furnished; there were a few chairs, a dressing-table and a large double bed. On one of the chairs lay the red silk dress that was too indecent for her to entertain in, and sitting up in the bed was Nancy Kang herself. She held a flimsy sheet up to cover her breasts, but her shoulders and arms were naked. The red lips were smiling and the gleam was back in her eyes.

She seemed unaware that there was anything amiss with the way he had burst into the room. She simply smiled and waited.

Larren walked towards her and handed her the glass, his face was expressionless. She accepted it and sipped without speaking. Her mocking eyes were fixed on Larren's face. Then she emptied her glass and let it fall to the floor. Calmly she let the single sheet slide from her fingers and settle with a soft whisper around her waist. She was naked and her arms reached out for him, her fingers closing gently over his bandaged wrists. When she spoke her voice was a low, throaty whisper.

"Isn't this what you wanted?"

Larren stared down at her, his grey-green eyes roving over the cream-white lines of her body. Long ago he had lost the ability to answer a woman's love, for his heart had frozen and died on the same dark night that his adored Andrea had been murdered; but he had never lost the lust for a woman's body. When Nancy Kang fell back upon the bed and pulled him down on top of her he came willingly.

Her arms locked around his shoulders, holding him against her as her mouth sought his lips. His left hand closed over the hard curve of her right shoulder, his right hand over the infinitely softer curve of her left breast. She gasped beneath him as his weight crushed her, but still her mouth clamped hungrily against his own. They were locked together by a kiss that burned like a flame between them. Her right hand slipped away from his shoulder and Larren barely felt it go, her left arm still held him down tightly against her. Then suddenly he felt the muscles knotting hard in the soft body beneath him and in the same moment he saw that her eyes were still open and gleaming viciously. In that moment he knew the nature of the trap he had suspected all along; and he knew too that the flame of desire between them burned only on one side. He thrust her hard down on the bed and tore himself away from her embrace in the same instant that the knife that had appeared in her right hand sliced past his stomach.

The razor-edged blade actually ripped through the cloth of his jacket as he pushed his body away and Nancy Kang screamed in a mixture of baffled rage and the crushing pain where his hands still pressed down on her shoulder and breast.

She kicked clear of the sheet and attempted to lunge at him again but he caught her wrist and gave it a twist. She screamed again as the knife fell from her fingers and Larren scooped it up from the bed beside her. Her nude limbs threshed wildly but Larren held her down.

He said savagely, "So you are working for Dressler. Where is he now?"

Nancy Kang answered him by arching her lovely body and spitting viciously in his face.

CHAPTER 13: DISCOVERY OF A CORPSE

Nancy Kang's nylon stockings lay with her red dress across the back of the bedside chair and Larren used one of them to lash her wrists together. He had great difficulty in holding her as she clawed and bit at him in a writhing fury, but at last he managed to roll her over on to her face and secure one wrist at a time while he knelt with one knee in the small of her back to hold her down. When he eased his weight off her she twisted over and kicked out wildly with her legs until he succeeded in restraining those also and knotted the other stocking about her trim ankles.

At last he stood back from the bed, the side of his face and the backs of his hands were marked with scratches and tiny pinpoints of blood where she had scored with her nails and teeth, and he was breathing heavily as he stared down at her. Her smooth body arched and contorted as she strained against her bonds, and he could see the swell and ripple of her muscles moving beneath her naked flesh. She stopped her struggles suddenly and began to curse him in a virulent stream of Cantonese.

Larren ignored her and turned to make a brief but thorough search of the bedroom. The only thing of interest that he was able to uncover, however, was the leather sheath that had held the knife with which the cursing dancer had tried to kill him; it was strapped to the leg of the bed where it was hidden below the hanging coverlet, and positioned so that she only had to reach down her arm as she lay back on the bed to reach the concealed blade.

Larren eyed the sheath and the knife and then looked back at the woman.

He said grimly, "I've heard of people being cold-blooded, but this is going to take some beating. How many more men have you lured in here and then knifed as they lay on top of you?"

Nancy bared her teeth at him and burst into another maddened fit of writhing.

Larren waited until she had relaxed again and then stood over her with the knife. Gently he pricked the point of the blade into her stomach just below the navel, and there was a grimly detached look about his unsmiling mouth and grey-green eyes.

He said softly, "You work for Dressler, don't you?"

"I work for the Communist party — and for Red Hatchet Tong."

"And what is the connection between the two?"

"Find out for yourself."

She screamed the last phrase at him and arched her body upwards in a suicidal effort to thrust her stomach against the knife. Larren drew the blade back only just in time and left nothing more than a slight gash in the soft flesh. Nancy swore at him again and Larren knew that he would learn nothing more from her; she had just proved that she would sooner die than talk.

Without wasting any more time on the dancer Larren returned to the living-room and used her telephone to dial Naval Headquarters in Victoria. He turned the knife over in his hands as he waited and finally tossed it on to a nearby table when he heard Kendall answer.

He said wearily, "It's Larren here, Commander. I'm speaking from Nancy Kang's apartment. The woman has just admitted that she works for both Dressler and the tong, but I'm afraid she's still a dead lead. You can send somebody over to pick her up, but she won't talk."

Kendall answered slowly, "I don't think it matters now, Larren. It's too late. I was just on my way to answer a call from Superintendent Chappel of the Hong Kong police; one of his Chinese policemen discovered a corpse floating in the harbour half an hour ago. The body hasn't been positively identified yet, but he's pretty sure that it's Maclean's."

The body was Maclean's.

Larren, Kendall, Superintendent Chappel and a police doctor all stood in a grim circle around the long table in the police mortuary, the doctor raised the sheet over the body and Kendall nodded slowly.

The doctor said quietly, "I'd say he had been in the water for several hours before he was picked up. He died from a bullet in the back of his head." He drew the sheet back a little farther and said, "The only thing that puzzles me are these tiny little pinpricks that are dotted over his body, as you can see by the smears of blood over his chest they are pretty plentiful." He scowled. "Perhaps the autopsy can tell us."

Larren said flatly, "I can tell you now." He was aware of the three men looking up at him as he went on. "Those tiny holes were made by a thin needle-like instrument like a very fine screwdriver. The needle is pushed in and then scraped along the bone, the effect is pretty gruesome."

The doctor said slowly, "How can you tell?"

"I've seen it used before. It's Franz Reutall's favourite method of torture." He stopped for a moment and then added: "He once used it on me."

Kendall swore softly but nobody else spoke. Instead they stared down at the marks of torture on the dead man's body. At last the doctor replaced the sheet.

They left the doctor and the corpse in the cold, white-tiled room and thankfully made their way back to the outer office. There Larren and Kendall parted from the Superintendent who promised to keep them informed of any new developments. They thanked the beefy man for his help and then returned to the large black car that Kendall had waiting outside.

They were silent for a half mile or so as their driver cruised the car through the noisy streets. Then Larren said bitterly:

"I suppose it was my fault, Commander. I could have rescued him from that junk if I hadn't acted on a stupid impulse to save Maxine Kia's useless neck."

"No, Larren." Kendall pulled himself out of his lethargy of despair to answer, "You can't blame yourself for that." He leaned forward in his seat and went on grimly. "Besides, now that we know that he's dead, that part of it is all over. The problem now is pure and simple — how much did he tell them?"

"He may not have told them anything."

"Don't be a fool!" Kendall spoke the words angrily but almost immediately he clamped his emotions under control again. He went on more quietly. "He didn't die on them, Larren, he was shot."

"Not necessarily. Dressler and Reutall have broken away from the tong, remember. The tong was hiding them out before, but now that Dressler has turned them against him they may have made things too hot for him. It's possible that he and Reutall may have had to get rid of Maclean fast in order to escape back into China before getting decorated with a couple of those fancy hatchets."

Kendall said slowly, "That's possible, but even if that was the case I think they would have tried to smuggle Maclean away with them. They wouldn't have got rid of him until they had got what they wanted. But was Maclean able to satisfy them merely with *Vigilant*'s position — or was he forced to reveal that Mason's strike party was on the mainland as well?"

Larren couldn't answer that, but after a thoughtful pause Kendall spoke again.

"Maclean knew that the important thing was to make sure that the Communists don't get even the glimmer of suspicion about the strike party," he mused. "So he would definitely attempt to make Dressler believe that *Vigilant*'s position was the only thing that he could tell them." He swung round suddenly on Larren. "You know Dressler better than anyone else, do you think Maclean could have convinced him?"

Larren grimaced. "It's hard to say because I don't know Maclean. But I do know that anyone would have a hard task in fooling Dressler. The man's as cold as a dead fish and as heartless as a block of solid stone, and if he only suspected that Maclean was holding something back he would let Reutall continue his sadistic little experiments."

Kendall wiped a smear of perspiration away from his temples with the back of his hand and shifted his weight uncomfortably in the close interior of the car. His responsibilities weighed down upon him like an invisible shroud.

He said desperately, "If only we knew where to find those two murdering friends of yours."

Larren answered him bleakly. "Whatever happened they're probably back over the frontier by now. They wouldn't risk staying in Hong Kong with both the police and the tong killers looking for them."

"You're most likely right, now that Maclean's dead they've got nothing to keep them here, they'll have gone back to report."

Larren hesitated. "What happens if Maclean did spill everything?" he queried at last. "Is there anything we can do to help Mason and his party?"

"There's nothing," Kendall almost snarled. "Nothing that will do any good. I'll see that they're warned when they next make radio contact with *Watchful*, but that won't be until dawn tomorrow, and even if they're still free they won't stand any chance of escaping the net once a real search for them gets under way. If Maclean has told everything, then I'm afraid that Paul Mason and his companions have nothing better to look forward to than the inside of a Chinese prison."

It was not until the early hours of the following morning that Larren finally returned to his hotel. He had spent the whole day with Kendall desperately trying to find some lead that might take them to Dressler, for even though they were almost certain that both Dressler and Reutall were out of their reach they still had to consider the remote possibility that the two men just might have remained in Hong Kong. However, they had achieved nothing. They had badgered the unfortunate Superintendent Chappel into re-questioning every known friend of the dead tong man Cheng Kia in the hope of getting another lead to the missing Maxine, but it had proved to be a waste of their time and his. They had also checked on the movements of every other known Communist agent, or suspected agent, in the twin cities of Hong Kong and Kowloon with equally negative results. And finally they had both visited the jail cell where Nancy Kang was being held, and had received only a fresh string of filthy curses for their pains.

After that they had had no choice but to give up. Kendall had returned to Naval Headquarters in order to receive the latest signal from Mason as soon as it came through, and Larren had decided to snatch a few hours' sleep before he was needed again. His headache had returned and he knew that he needed a stiff drink and some rest to clear his mind properly.

The desk clerk gave him a sleepy nod as he entered the hotel and climbed the stairs. His room was on the first floor and he paused outside the door to fumble for his key. He twisted the key in the lock and pushed the door open, and as he crossed the threshold his hand reached for the light switch. Before he could find it a massive arm locked swiftly around his throat.

Larren choked hoarsely as the giant figure who had stepped from behind the door dragged him bodily into the room. In the same moment he saw a second dark shape in front of him and then the door was closed behind him and the room was pitch black.

The ferocious armlock on his neck was unbreakable, and before he really had a chance to fight back his left arm was being twisted up behind his back in an equally solid grip.

Then the light clicked on and he saw the slight, ponytailed figure of Maxine facing him with a revolver in her slim hand.

The powerful giant that held him was the Mongol Kolo.

CHAPTER 14: SILENCE

Larren relaxed slowly in the fast grip of the Mongol's embrace, and for the moment he was unable to move. Maxine was watching him with a wary look in her dark eyes, her small hand held the gun pointing steadily at his middle but the expression on her fragile face was momentarily undecided.

Then suddenly she said, "Release him, Kolo."

The Mongol hesitated and then slackened his grip on Larren's arm and throat. Maxine gave him a sharp look and somewhat reluctantly he stepped back out of the way.

Larren drew a deep breath and gingerly explored around his throat with his fingers. The massive Kolo was watching him closely with obvious distrust; he was wearing a cheap shirt and a pair of normal trousers, and he looked somewhat clumsy compared to the picture he had presented in the brief loincloth when he had attempted to kill Larren at the tong temple at Cheng Kia's home. The bald dome of his head was shining beneath the electric light above him, and his solid features looked strangely petulant, as though he had hoped that Maxine would give him another chance to use his bare and murderous hands.

Maxine said quietly, "I came to thank you, Simon, for saving my life aboard the junk."

Larren looked at the revolver in her hand and then at the waiting Mongol.

"Is that all?"

"No." Her face was troubled and she came slightly nearer. "I also came to warn you, to give you a chance to save your friends. The man named Maclean broke down under Reutall's torturing, and he told them that there are five men on the mainland of China who are trying to reach your sunken submarine and destroy the most important pieces of her equipment. So now Dressler and Reutall have gone back to China to make sure that your friends are either captured or killed."

Larren's unsmiling mouth became a fraction harder as he looked into her dark eyes, and something in the unflinching sadness that he saw there told him that she spoke the truth. He suddenly knew too that she would not use the gun, and he turned and took a few paces to the small table that held his medicinal whisky. Kolo tensed eagerly, but when he received no sign from Maxine he relaxed.

Larren poured himself a large, neat drink and poured it down his throat in one long movement. *So now we know*, he thought bitterly, *Mason and his men are walking right into a trap.* He turned very slowly to face Maxine again and said:

"Thank you, Maxine. But why the gun?"

She said slowly, "The police are searching for me because of my activities with Red Hatchet Tong. Your people want me too."

He shrugged. "You can put it away. I won't turn you in."

Her eyes studied him for a few moments and then she abruptly lowered the gun. She had a small handbag in her free hand and she slipped the gun inside and snapped the clasp shut. Then she looked at him again. Her face was lightly powdered and she wore another high-necked dress with the traditional slit up one thigh. She waited silently for him to speak.

He said at last, "How can you be sure that Maclean told everything? I thought that you had finished with Dressler."

"I was not finished — if I could have found him I would have killed him." Her voice was cold and hard. "However, I could not find out where he had gone. He fled from the junk and vanished completely. I would not know now what had happened if he had not taken Kolo with him."

Larren spared another glance for her silent bodyguard, and when he turned his gaze back to Maxine he found that she had moved suddenly closer.

She said hesitantly. "Kolo was ashore when you and I fled from the junk, and when he returned Dressler was preparing to move." She looked into Larren's face as though she half expected him to disbelieve her story and went on. "Dressler needed Kolo's strength to help him to carry Maclean away, so he told him that you had escaped and that Tao Shen and I were chasing you. He also claimed that I had said that Kolo was to follow his orders, so my poor Kolo obeyed him."

Larren suddenly realised that she was concerned for the giant, and was trying to clear him of any blame over Maclean's death.

"They ordered Kolo to carry Maclean aboard an empty sampan." Maxine fidgeted as she spoke. "Then Kolo poled them out into the harbour and they sailed to some other junk shelter in one of the bays around the New Territories. He was there when they tortured Maclean and he heard Maclean tell them all that he knew. Then Dressler shot your friend and dumped the body in the harbour. They sailed back into the bay and Dressler spoke of returning to China and settling with your other friends."

Maxine faltered again and then said, "It was after this that Kolo began to realise that all was not well. He could not understand why neither I nor Tao Shen had returned. So when Reutall and Dressler left him he found his way back to Kowloon, and from there he went to another of our concealed temples. The guardians there knew where to find me and I hurried over there to fetch him. I made him tell me all that he could remember, and then I came over here to warn you."

Larren said slowly, "Is he certain that Dressler and Reutall have already left Hong Kong?"

"He is as certain as it is possible for him to be. His is a devoted servant. He has protected me ever since I was a child. He did nothing to help your Commander Maclean because he was told that I wished him to obey Dressler." She licked her lips delicately and added, "Kolo is not really cruel, he has nothing but his great strength and he enjoys the use of his muscles, but he would not harm anyone unless I ordered it."

Larren slowly poured himself another drink, he was not particularly interested in Kolo and his mind was busy with the problem of Reutall and Dressler. He wanted those two men badly — wanted to watch them die as Andrea had died — and now the thought that they had again escaped him stirred a pool of bitterness inside him. He threw the drink back angrily and suddenly decided to get drunk.

Maxine's hand closed with an unexpected firmness over his wrist as he reached again for the bottle, and he hesitated, looking into her eyes and finding them again filled with sadness.

She said softly: "Is there anything I can do to help?"

Larren said nothing, but he made no effort to resist as she pulled his hand away from the whisky bottle. He thought of Andrea again, but forced himself to recognise that there were stronger, living loyalties that must be placed above his own dark vendetta; he still had a job to do for Alan Kendall.

He cleared his mind and looked down at Maxine.

"It might help if you could tell me how the tong came to be mixed up with Dressler and Reutall?"

For a moment it seemed that he had asked the wrong question, one that she would refuse to answer.

But at last she said:

"It was through my brother Cheng, he was a leader of the tong but in the last few years he had also become a firm Communist. Cheng was an idealist who could see only the hopeless dreams of Communism and not the stark realities. He began to use his power as a tong man to help the Communists, and at first there was big trouble between him and other leaders of the tong. Then Dressler came, and brought with him flowery promises to say that in return for help now the leaders of Red Hatchet Tong would be granted high places in the new government when the British lease expires and the Chinese regain Hong Kong; the sons of Red Hatchet Tong would wield the same power as our fathers and with these promises Cheng gained the support of the tong for Dressler."

Maxine drew an angry breath and added vehemently. "It was a black day for us when we listened to Dressler. Now my brother Cheng is dead; Tao Shen is dead; the police are forcing us back underground; and we now know that Dressler's word meant nothing."

Larren said slowly, "I'm sorry." He listened to his own words and realised that it was incredible that he should be standing here and expressing sympathy with the ritual killers who had butchered Maclean's wife, daughter and servants. But as far as Maxine Kia was concerned he knew that he was sincere.

Maxine sensed something of his thoughts for she said in a low voice. "Perhaps I am a bad woman for owing loyalty to the tong; but both my father and my brother were powerful tong men, and the vivid words of men who can speak well can make any action — even murder — seem justified when it is done to aid a political ideal."

Larren's mind strayed back to the dark days of 1944 when he too had butchered with a knife while in enemy territory, and he knew that he of all people could pass no judgment on Maxine Kia. He said simply:

"What you have told me may be of help to Lieutenant-Commander Kendall, and I'll pass it on. At least we now know for certain that Dressler has gone back to China, and that'll save us from chasing our tails around Hong Kong. I wish I knew how to thank you."

Maxine hesitated, the deep gaze of her dark eyes searching his face. Then she turned to face the waiting Mongol.

"Go outside, Kolo. Wait for me there," she ordered quietly.

The Mongol stared at her and then turned his resentful eyes towards Larren.

"It's all right, Kolo. I shall be quite safe."

Slowly the giant turned away and went to the door. He stopped there and looked back over his shoulder, the perspiration glistened on the gleaming dome of his head and his eyes held a look of distrust. He shook his head uncomprehendingly and then obediently closed the door behind him.

Larren remained waiting as Maxine moved close against him.

"Simon," she faltered. "There is so much that I have to thank you for too."

Without waiting for an answer she swept her arms around his neck and stood on tiptoe to find his mouth with her lips. Larren held her gently, feeling her arms link behind him as her slim body trembled in his arms. Her seeking lips were soft and pliant under his own and her eyes were closed below the light arc of her brows. She answered his returning kiss with a feverish intensity that gave an unexpected strength and suppleness to her tightly-clinging body, and slowly his arms lost their gentleness as he crushed her against his chest.

"Simon —" she moaned his name fretfully through their kiss — "Simon — Oh, Simon…"

Larren's hand moved lightly in responsive searching, caressing the trembling lines of her shoulders and tracing the soft contours of her body. He felt the smooth flesh of her thigh where her dress was slit above the top of her stocking and his touch sent a shiver of ecstasy throughout her limbs.

Their mouths parted for an instant and she pleaded huskily:

"Take me, Simon. If you want me, take me. Dressler would have killed me if you had not saved me from him, and I owe you everything. Everything, Simon, my body, heart and soul."

His fingers found the zip that released her dress and he pulled it down, and as the material fell away from her shoulders the begging eagerness of her taut body told him that it was more than gratitude that spurred her on. There was nothing submissive or dutiful about her approach, there was just a raw and striving hunger; she needed him far more than he needed her.

However, as the dress settled in a whispering heap on the floor, Larren swung one arm beneath her knees and lifted her up. He had to push the bedroom door open with his knee and her lips were still locked against his own as he carried her inside.

Larren's head was again aching when he returned to Naval Headquarters a few hours later, and he tried unsuccessfully to convince himself that the episode with Maxine Kia had refreshed him as much as would the brief sleep he had intended to snatch. Now he had to report to Alan Kendall.

The young Lieutenant-Commander had moved permanently into the office that had been Maclean's, and Larren found him slumped wearily behind his big desk. He looked up as Larren came in and Larren saw lines of tiredness etched around the other's face; Kendall had obviously had no sleep either.

"Any developments?" Larren asked.

Kendall shook his head. "I'm waiting for *Watchful* to report by radio. They'll warn Mason of what's happened here when he contacts them — that's if he's still in any position to make contact."

Larren sat down and quietly outlined all that Maxine had told him. Kendall listened, his face growing gradually harder.

At last the Naval man said, "It's no more than we expected. It was futile of us to hope otherwise."

There was silence in the large office, and neither man was willing to break it. They had failed Mason and his men and there was nothing to say that would have any point or meaning. Outside the large window the dawn was breaking, a dim fading of the darkness that failed to bring any cheer into the room where the two men sat.

Then abruptly the door opened and they both looked round as a secretary came towards them. She held a slip of white paper in her hand and her face was grave.

She said quietly, "This signal was just received from *Watchful*, Commander."

Kendall took the white paper from her hand. He read it through and then glanced up to find Larren watching him. In a flat, emotionless voice he read the signal aloud.

"From submarine *Watchful* to Naval Headquarters, Hong Kong. We regret to inform you that there is complete radio silence from Captain Mason and his party. Their signal is now two hours' overdue. We will maintain a radio alert."

Kendall dropped the signal on to the desk and repeated bitterly: "Complete radio silence."

CHAPTER 15: MIDNIGHT LANDING

The brief signal from *Watchful* set the final seal of gloom upon the rigid atmosphere of the large room. The secretary hesitated for a moment and then tactfully and quietly withdrew. The two men were left alone with their thoughts.

Kendall stared down at the white paper on his desk. His expression was one of savage helplessness and his clenched fists were a line of white patches along the knuckles. There was bitterness and self-condemnation in his eyes and it was clear that he regarded Mason and his men as already dead.

Larren was reluctant to give them up so quickly.

He said, "They may still be free, Commander. You told me that the last time they made contact with *Watchful* they were having trouble with their radio. It may be that their set has broken down."

"So what? The fact still remains that we can't warn them, and even if we could it will still be a mere matter of time. The success of their mission depended on total secrecy; we knew all along that the Chinese could soon draft enough men into the area to hunt them down if their presence once became known. And now that Dressler and Reutall have returned to China to organise the search —"

He didn't bother to finish; it wasn't necessary.

However, Larren was still unwilling to leave the problem alone. He had never met Paul Mason or any of his party but he found that he could not mentally abandon them to their plight. His head began to throb again beneath the patch of plaster that still adorned the back of his skull as he twisted the possibilities around in his mind.

At last he said slowly, "Wouldn't it be possible for *Watchful* to take them off? I know you can't send her in to pick them up, but they're all strong swimmers and they should be capable of swimming out past the twelve mile limit."

Kendall shook his head. "It's not as easy as you seem to think to spot a man swimming in the open sea. Mason and his men would have to get well clear of the twelve mile limit before *Watchful* would dare surface to pick them up, and by that time they would be near exhausted and could easily drown. Besides which, you seem to have forgotten the fact that we can't get in touch with them anyway."

"But if it was possible to contact Mason, could you have *Watchful* surface to pick them up? It would give them a better chance than they'll have with the Chinese."

Kendall said warily, "I could order *Watchful* to make an attempt at picking them up, but the problem is that the Chinese would probably disregard their own limits and still attack her. They still have their destroyers patrolling the whole length of that coastline, and we'd be as near as dammit to their waters anyway. The whole operation would be too risky and I doubt if I'd get permission to chance losing another submarine."

Kendall spoke as though he was uttering the final seal to the conversation, but after a short lull he looked up again.

"How were you going to contact Mason anyway?"

Larren said calmly, "If *Watchful* can surface to pick five men up then she can surface to put one man down — me. I may not be a champion but I think I could make the swim to the shore."

Kendall looked at him as though he had gone mad.

"Now that is crazy. There's a big difference between landing men and picking them up. For one thing *Watchful* is certain to be spotted by one of those destroyers when she surfaces, and that means that the Chinese would be waiting with open arms to greet you as you land. And if we were to land you below the area patrolled by the destroyers as we did Mason's party then you would have a five-night hike to catch them up."

Larren grimaced as he realised that the Naval man was right: the Chinese would obviously be alerted by the sight of the submarine, and although this would not matter when picking Mason up, provided that they got away before the Chinese could react, it would be fatal for any man they tried to land.

They lapsed into another sombre silence that was not broken until the outer door opened again after another almost inaudible knock. The secretary entered again holding an identical slip of white paper and said quietly:

"A second signal from *Watchful*, sir."

Kendall accepted the signal and this time he remembered to dismiss her. He read the flimsy paper through and then stared at Larren with a flicker of new interest in his eyes.

"The Chinese have withdrawn their destroyers," he said slowly. "There's now only one vessel left, and that's stationed directly over *Vigilant* at Disaster Point. You know what that means?"

"It means that Dressler and Reutall have got back to report *Vigilant*'s position."

"Obviously, now that they know *Vigilant*'s precise location they only need one ship to keep watch over her and they don't have to patrol the whole coastline. But what it really means is that it would be possible to land you much nearer to Disaster Point now that the search has been called off. Mason and his party should be lying up approximately eighteen to twenty miles south of Disaster Point and we could set you down within a few miles of —" He broke off suddenly and swore.

Larren knew what had just crossed Kendall's mind, but he waited for the man to speak. Kendall's face had clouded with sudden, bitter anger and at last he said slowly:

"I'm a fool, for a moment I had forgotten that the fact that Dressler has obviously passed on his report means that the search for Mason must even now be at its height. We couldn't possibly land anyone on the mainland until after nightfall tonight and by then it will be too late for a warning to be of any use. Even if their radio has broken down and they are still free they won't possibly be able to evade capture until then."

"They just might," Larren argued. "Maclean can only have told Dressler that they are somewhere along the eighty-mile stretch of coastline between Disaster Point and Tung Chu Bay where they were landed. That's a lot of coastline to be searched, and it will take time for the Chinese to get a large number of men moved into the area. Mason and his men just might be able to stay free until tonight."

Kendall shook his head. "I can't agree, Larren. The Chinese will know from Maclean how long Mason and his men have been on the mainland, and they can work out within a little how far the strike party could have travelled. I'm afraid that there's still nothing that we can do for them — and they knew that when they volunteered for this mission."

"All right," Larren said harshly. "We'll assume that even if Mason and his men are free now they must inevitably be in Chinese hands by nightfall. But the last thing that the Chinese will expect then is for another landing on their territory. It may be possible to release Mason and company and get them aboard *Watchful* before the hue and cry can get going again. We've got to try."

Kendall's gaze fixed on Larren's hard, grey-green eyes.

He said, "You're pretty determined to shove your head into the same noose as Mason's aren't you?"

Larren said grimly, "I feel vaguely responsible for them. If I hadn't bungled things aboard the junk I might have succeeded in getting Maclean away and avoided all this."

Kendall drew an angry breath. "You feel responsible for them," he ejaculated. "How the hell do you think I feel?"

"I don't give a damn what you feel," Larren snapped back. "I just want to salvage something from a job I've messed up — namely five men's lives."

Kendall glared at him for a moment and then suddenly he kicked his chair back and stalked over to the map of the Chinese coastline that hung on the wall. He jabbed his finger against a spot south of Disaster Point and said flatly,

"If we take an average of the mileage they covered on the first three nights they should be somewhere here. I can lay on a seaplane to take you north and rendezvous with *Watchful* in the Yellow Sea. Tonight you can be landed on this stretch of coast after dark." He spun round to face Larren. "You'll have to take another man with you though — a Chinese who can enter one of the villages and fish for information. If it's possible to bring off a rescue do so, but if Mason's party is under too heavy a guard you'll return to *Watchful* and give up the idea. Will that satisfy you?"

Larren said quietly, "It will."

Kendall came back to the desk and stood beside it.

"I'll fix you up with a radio," he said more soberly, "so you can maintain contact with *Watchful* once you're ashore. I think I can arrange for you to have a set with a waterproof casing so you can call up the submarine while you're swimming. You'll also have a flare gun to enable her to pick you up once you get out of the twelve mile limit."

Larren stood up and said, "Thanks, you won't regret it."

"I'd better not. Now you get the hell out of here and grab yourself some sleep while I try to sell this hare-brained scheme to my superiors."

Larren turned to go but the tall Lieutenant-Commander held him back for just a few seconds longer. He held out his hand and said quietly:

"Don't get yourself killed, Larren. I can't afford to lose any more good men over this affair."

Larren clasped his hand and replied,

"I'll do my best, Commander. With luck I'll bring a few of those men back to base yet."

The man whom Kendall had approached to accompany Larren into China was an unimpressive young man named Johnny Ling. He was of intermediate height and wiry build, and his smile was an ever-flickering gleam of white teeth in an otherwise unremarkable face. He looked like any other young Chinese man who could be found in the streets of Victoria or Kowloon, but his looks were a poor advertisement for his capabilities. Johnny Ling had a fanatical hatred for the Communists; and the Communists had set a high price upon his sleek black head.

Larren watched him as they sat opposite each other in the officers' wardroom of the submarine *Watchful*. They had met in Kendall's office after the Intelligence man had won a hard-fought battle with his superiors to obtain the co-operation of *Watchful* on their mission, and Larren had decided immediately that Johnny Ling was the right man for the job. Now he said curiously:

"What made you volunteer for this job, Johnny?"

The smile flickered. "Why do you ask that?"

"Because Kendall told me that the Communists will probably have your back to a firing squad wall if they ever catch you, and that ought to have given you more reason than anybody else to back off. I might get away with a prison sentence, but not you."

Johnny Ling said softly, "That is so, but you cannot fight Communism by running away from it. There is also another reason, one of those men with Captain Mason is a close friend of mine, his name is Fen Liu."

Larren said slowly, "Now I understand."

Johnny's eyes still held Larren's face.

"And you, Mr. Larren, why are you so willing to risk the possible feel of the firing squad wall against your back?"

Larren shrugged. "It's partly my fault that Mason is in this mess, so I guess I owe it to him to try and get him out."

Johnny smiled and shook his head. "There is another reason."

Larren looked up in surprise. "What does that mean?"

"It means that I saw the look on your face when we first met in Commander Kendall's office; the look that came when he mentioned two men with the names Reutall and Dressler. There was vengeance in your eyes, Mr. Larren, not concern for Mason and his men."

Larren suddenly knew that Johnny was right; he would do all he could for Mason's strike party, but at the same time they were simply an excuse; an excuse to follow his wife's murderers into Communist China. Subconsciously he must have known it all along, but it had taken Johnny Ling to make him accept it clearly.

He said at last, "Don't let it bother you, Johnny. Mason and company come first — I'm just hoping that those other two will get in my way."

Johnny Ling's teeth flickered in an uncaring smile and they both allowed the subject to drop.

A few minutes later *Watchful*'s Captain came into the wardroom. He was a bulky, blue-jawed man who wasted few words and approached everything with an air of solid determination. His name was Allendale.

He said briskly, "It's half an hour to midnight and we're now approaching the twelve mile boundary. It's time you were moving."

Larren stood up. "Thanks, we'll get our gear together."

Allendale waved him down.

"Wait a minute," he said purposely. "I've been doing some thinking. If you characters are capable of getting out of the escape hatch I can take you in a lot closer. I daren't surface inside the twelve mile limit, but now that those destroyers have stopped patrolling I can get closer underwater. I can get you within a couple of miles and open the hatch at periscope depth."

"I'll try it." Larren looked at Johnny.

The Chinese man nodded. "I always did hate long swims."

"Well you'll have to have one coming back because I can't take you aboard without coming to the surface, but I can certainly let you out. Come for'd with me and I'll get one of the Petty Officers to give you some escape drill while we sneak closer along the bottom."

He turned briskly away and both Larren and Johnny Ling had to jump up smartly to catch up with him as he led them out into the steel-walled corridor.

Just over half an hour later two heads burst out of the dark surface of the sea, bobbing like pieces of flotsam among the low waves. Above the sky was cloudy and only a few stars penetrated the blanket of night. Less than a mile away was the almost undistinguishable silhouette of the Chinese shore. Simon Larren shook the water from his eyes and spat out the unaccustomed mouthpiece of his breathing apparatus, and still shivering from the bitter shock of being ejected out into the cold water he began to swim towards the second piece of flotsam that was Johnny Ling.

Somewhere underneath them, just below the surface, lay *Watchful*, but there was nothing now to tell them that she was still there for even her periscope was lowered. Larren reached Johnny Ling through a slapping wave that washed salt water up his nose and saw that the Chinese man was still smiling despite the chattering of his teeth.

"This is too cold for comfort," complained Ling.

Larren agreed with him and together they struck out strongly for the shore. Allendale, they knew, would give them a few minutes grace to get clear before taking his submarine back outside the twelve mile limit.

Each of them carried a waterproof pack on their shoulders as they swam; Larren's contained their radio transmitter, two revolvers, and his precious sheath knife which had been returned to him by Maxine Kia; Johnny Ling's pack contained dry clothing for them to change into once they reached the shore. Both packs began to grow infinitely heavier long before they reached the end of their swim, and Larren muttered a brief prayer of thanks for Allendale's assistance in bringing his submarine so far into Chinese waters.

At last, however, the shoreline gradually became nearer, clarifying into a dark ridge of rugged hills. They heard the soft booming of the sea upon the shore, and finally Larren's knees grazed on the gravelly bottom.

He stood up and staggered forwards with the waves breaking and rolling around his thighs. Johnny straightened up beside him and together they walked up the beach.

They were both panting hard for breath, and the night air struck with a vicious chill through their sodden clothing. They had borrowed thick sweaters and trousers from some of the members of *Watchful*'s crew to keep in some of their body heat as they swam, but now the wind was ripping through the thick wool.

Swiftly they stripped down, their teeth chattering and their bodies seized by a spate of shivering. Johnny Ling knelt to tear open the waterproof pack he had carried and fumbled uncontrollably as he drew out dry clothing and a rough towel. They towelled themselves dry and dressed hurriedly, still shaking from the bitter chill.

Once they had dressed Larren moved farther up the beach and quickly scraped a hole in the sand with his hands to bury the two sets of breathing apparatus and the wet clothing they had discarded. Johnny helped him to bury them and they smoothed the sand back into place. Then Larren swung his own pack with the radio transmitter back on to his shoulders and with Johnny leading the way they hurried up the beach.

They moved fast, as much to keep warm as to get away before they were seen.

CHAPTER 16: CALCULATED RISK

The terrain sloped up steeply from the sea, a climbing, sandy surface that was tufted with wiry clumps of long grass and a few low, stunted bushes. The night was very dark and they could distinguish nothing of their surroundings except the occasional ridges of rock that would loom suddenly in front of them. Behind and below them there were the almost imperceptible gleams of breaking water where the wave-caps tumbled in from the sea, but soon a sudden dip in the ground ahead swallowed them up and cut even that from their view.

It was not long before the ground began to rise again, becoming less sandy and more barren. They climbed higher into the rugged hill range that paralleled the coastline, and they grew slowly warmer from the heat of their exertions. Neither of them spoke; Johnny Ling picked their path with a confident sureness, as though he had spent every night of his life in moving about strange country in pitch darkness; Larren followed him with the unhesitating trust that the Chinese man inspired.

They pushed on without a pause for two to three hours, getting steadily higher above sea level, the range of hills closed around them and their legs began to ache slightly from the strain. The air was damp and misty, but now that their eyes had become accustomed to the gloom they could make out the black outline of the encircling heights which were just visible against the lesser darkness of the sky. The terrain was growing more rugged and the grass tufts and small bushes were no longer to be seen. There was nothing but black ridges of rock and barren hills.

At last, after tackling the steepest incline they had yet faced, they entered a narrow gap that was sunk between the sharply rising summits of two hills. Here Johnny Ling suddenly raised his hand and both men stopped. Ahead there were no more black outlines to indicate more hills, there was just darkness that obscured both earth and sky, showing no sign of where one began and the other ended. Silently Larren moved up to stand by Johnny's side.

The young man said quietly, "We are through the chain of hills that guard the coastline, and down below us there should be a flat plain of smallholdings and rice fields, and somewhere the village of Chushan. When it is daylight I will go down into the village and find out what I can about Mason and his party. If they have been captured anywhere within this area the villagers will know."

Larren said softly, "If they haven't been caught yet they will still be in these hills."

"They have been caught." Johnny was definite. "If they were still free these hills would be swarming with soldiers looking for them. The fact that the hills are deserted means that the hunt has been called off. Mason and his party are either dead or prisoners."

Larren knew he was right and said, "Let's hope that they're prisoners, then we may be able to do something for them."

"Maybe." This time Ling was non-committal. "But now we had better lay up and wait for dawn — we can do nothing more until then."

They turned and retreated into the hills with Johnny still leading the way, and after half an hour's searching they stumbled into a nest of large boulders that would keep them hidden from any idle eyes once the sun arose. Larren unslung his pack and leaned back against a flat slab of rock, his legs stretched out before him on the ground. Johnny Ling sat facing him.

Larren flexed his shoulder muscles and remarked, "It's a pity that there are no trees about. I'd feel safer if we were hidden from the air as well."

Johnny shrugged. "China is very short of trees in many places. Some areas are vastly over-populated and the peasants have cut down all the trees to make firewood in the winter. They are never replaced and so many parts of the country are barren. This stretch of coastline is almost uninhabited because the ground is so inhospitable, but the people from the valleys farther inland will have stripped the region of wood. We may find a few small copses of golden larch or Chinese pines, but there will be no forests."

"It's remarkable that Mason and his men got this far without being spotted if the region is so thick with people," Larren commented. He was unfastening the straps of his pack as he spoke.

"It is only down in the plains and valleys that the farms and villages are so crowded," Johnny explained. "Mason has been keeping to this chain of half hills and half mountains that follows the sea. This part where we are now is the narrowest part of the chain, so you must not get the impression that it is only the few miles in width that we have covered tonight. In places this range is over twenty miles wide and everywhere it is too bleak and unyielding to be farmed; so, Mason has been able to keep between the plains and the fishing villages that live from the sea. He ran little risk of being seen as he was moving only at night, but at the same time it would not have taken many hours for the Chinese to flush his party out once they knew that they were here."

Larren smiled. "Thanks for the lesson in geography." He passed over one of the two slabs of chocolate he had fished from his pack, and with it a pint flask of brandy. "Here — have some of this."

Johnny accepted gratefully and they both made short work of the chocolate. They washed it down with warming mouthfuls of the fiery brandy, and then by mutual consent they relaxed in silence to wait for the dawn.

Larren closed his eyes but sleep would not come. His wrists were still bandaged from his adventure aboard the junk, and although the raw patches of skin no longer gave him any real trouble they were smarting from the salt water that had soaked through during his swim. Besides this minor discomfort he had slept through most of the day, first in his own hotel and then dozing again in the cockpit of the seaplane that had flown himself and Johnny north to board *Watchful* at sea, and now he found himself too wide awake to accept this last chance to rest. Johnny Ling did not stir, but Larren knew from his breathing that he too was awake and waiting.

Those last few hours to dawn dragged with interminable slowness, nothing disturbed the blackness of the night and the low ground mist gradually began to spread its creeping chill through their bodies. Larren resisted the growing temptation to finish off the flask of brandy and pulled his jacket tighter about his shoulders. Johnny lay still, stolidly concealing his own impatience.

At last the night began to fade, the blackness dissolved to greyness and the stark outlines of the hills behind them were rimmed with pale pink as the sun rose behind and below the mountainous chain. They waited until the sky had cleared to a watery blue and the last of the shadows had retreated to the deepest hollows in the rocks, and then they left their place of concealment and returned cautiously to the gap in the hills that looked down on to the inland plain.

A thin white mist still moved in a wispy shroud around them, but as they neared the top of the climb they rose above it. They moved even more warily as they passed between the crests of the two flanking hills, knowing that if they were seen they could be hunted down as quickly as Mason and his party had been. At last Johnny muttered a low warning and crouched low to cover the last few yards of the slope. He dropped flat at the top and Larren slipped down on to his stomach and wriggled forward to join him.

Below them the scene was exactly as Johnny had said it would be, the long slope of the hillside leading down through a series of dips and hollows to the broad, flat plain. Here and there small patches of the dawn mist still lay like low grey clouds across the earth but they were gradually becoming smaller. A narrow road ran across the floor of the plain, twisting untidily despite the almost perfect flatness of its surroundings. On each side of the road the land was sectioned off into green rice fields, furrowed by crude ploughs and separated by irrigation ditches. Scattered almost everywhere were rough stone farmhouses that were little more than hovels, most of them with an adjoining vegetable crop of potatoes and beans. There were a few outhouses to each farm and they could hear the faint grunting of pigs and the crow of a cockerel even from this distance. To their right were two or three small villages, mere tumbledown dwellings with an air of defiant poverty, and to their left a long arm-like ridge of the mountain chain extended out into the valley.

Larren took a pair of powerful binoculars from his pack and watched the individual farmhouses spring to life as he swept them slowly over the scene below.

Johnny Ling said quietly, "Chushan should be somewhere behind that ridge of hills to our left. It is the largest village in the area and will be the best place to pick up information."

Larren handed him the binoculars.

"You know the country, Johnny. If you want to circle round to there it's okay with me."

Johnny studied the plain below before answering, then he lowered the glasses and said:

"We'd best circle round before the sun drags too many coolies from their beds. We'll make for that hill to our left and you can remain there while I slip into Chushan. There is a small military barracks in the village and the odds are high that our friends will be there. There is nowhere else that they could be held safely unless they have been transported out of the area altogether."

Larren replaced his glasses in his case and said:

"You know this country pretty well, don't you?"

"A long time ago I lived not very far from here." Johnny Ling spoke grimly and for once his constant smile was hidden. "But that was before the Communists came. Fen Liu lived near me, which is why he was chosen to guide Mason. We were no more than boys then, and we both fought for the Nationalist army during the war of 1949. We were driven out, and this is the first time that either of us have returned."

Larren sensed that there was a longer story behind the hard face of the young man, but he had no time to hear it. Johnny turned and wormed his way down the slope until he could stand up out of sight of the plain, and Larren quickly followed him. Again Johnny led the way as they began to circle round through the hills towards the village of Chushan.

For the next two hours they worked their way through the rocks and passes of the barren hills. Both men were wearing soiled and drab jackets and trousers of cheap blue cloth, and on their heads they wore wide straw hats like shallow lampshades; the clothing was baggy and shapeless and from a distance even Larren could be mistaken for a local. However, the pack that Larren carried would have aroused the curiosity of any stray peasant they might have met, and Johnny took great care to pick a route that would keep them hidden for most of the way.

Eventually they came out on the ridge of connecting hills that had hid Chushan from their view and here they both moved with utmost care as they made their way to the highest vantage point along the protruding arm. Crouching low they reached the summit of the chain and flattened side by side in a low hollow. Larren again used his binoculars to sweep the surrounding territory.

To their left was Chushan, a larger, more sprawling township with graceful sloping roofs that gave it a slightly grander appearance than the smaller villages on the plain to their right. The town looked cleaner and not quite so closely packed, and winding through its centre was a small stream that came down from the hills. In places there were even clumps of green bamboo along the stream's banks. The road ran straight through the town and crossed the river by a steep stone bridge, and after leaving the town it curved in a wide loop around the steep hill where Larren and Johnny Ling were lying, passing through a narrow defile below them and then vanishing across the plain.

Johnny said quietly, "You see the ugly square building behind the town, that is the barrack block where our friends will be if they are here at all. Wait here for me while I pay a visit to the town and find out for sure."

Larren said evenly, "Don't take any risks, Johnny."

"I won't have to. If Mason's party are there then their capture will have caused plenty of speculation among the people. I have only to listen to the talk as I walk by." A smile flickered again across his face. "Don't worry my friend, I will be back."

A few seconds later he was gone and Larren watched his unimposing figure moving cautiously down the hill. He realised slowly that he hadn't even wished him luck.

It was noon before Johnny Ling returned. The time passed with an agonising slowness that gradually consumed Larren's patience and made his hands itch for action as he lay in the hollow on the hilltop. And when finally he did see the untidy figure of his companion returning up the hillside he drew a deep breath of relief. The waiting was over and now perhaps they could do something, and the thought made him wipe his palms slowly along his thighs in a gesture of anticipation.

Johnny Ling was in a hurry and moving fast, almost running up the steep slope. He was panting for breath and almost fell into the hollow where Larren waited as he stumbled over the crest of the hill. For a moment Larren thought that he was being followed and he half drew the revolver that was tucked into his belt, but a quick survey down the hillside revealed no signs of pursuit.

Johnny flopped down breathlessly and said:

"They — they are there, Larren — three of them."

"Only three?"

He nodded his sleek head and gulped for air at the same time. "Only three, Larren, one Chinese and two Englishmen. The other two were killed; they resisted arrest. It is common knowledge."

"Where are they?"

"In the barracks, as I thought. But we must act fast if we are to act at all." He had to stop and gasp for breath, but almost immediately he went on. "There is an armoured car coming for them some time this morning — they are to be transferred to a stronger prison in a larger town to the north."

"This morning! It's noon already!"

"I know. I know. But the car has not arrived yet." He gestured weakly with his hand. "Watch the barracks through your glasses. See if there is any activity."

Larren rolled back to the edge of the hollow and peered down into Chushan through his binoculars. He picked out the large barrack building and then swore as the powerful lenses brought the square parade ground beside it into close focus. A squat armoured car was waiting smack in the centre of the square.

Johnny Ling wormed into position beside him and Larren passed him the glasses without a word. Johnny's mouth tightened as he too picked out the ugly, squared shape of the car.

"We are too late," he snarled vehemently. "Too bloody late—" And he spat out a stream of foul Cantonese that almost matched the vocabulary that Larren had heard from Nancy Kang.

Larren reached for the glasses and Johnny released them after a moment's hesitation. Staring down into the barrack square Larren swept the glasses towards the buildings. He saw a small group of men coming out on to the square, most of them wore military uniforms and held rifles or sten guns, but the three men in the middle of the group walked with their hands behind their backs. Larren watched them move towards the armoured car, he was too far away to distinguish the features of any of the men but it was obvious that the prisoners were the survivors of Mason's party.

Grimly Larren gave the now silent Johnny Ling a verbal account of what was happening as the three prisoners were forced into the back of the car. Two of the guards climbed into the back with them, each clutching a sten gun beneath his right arm. The doors were slammed and then two more armed men swung into the front of the vehicle. One of them took the wheel and the car began to move out of the barrack square, through the wide gates and into the town of Chushan.

Larren left the car and followed the road it would have to travel with his glasses, the road that looped around their vantage point and vanished across the plain behind him.

He said hopefully, "Couldn't we ambush them as they pass through that gap in the hills below us?"

Johnny stirred beside him to study the point where the road wound through the narrow defile that cut through the chain of hills on which they were now lying. He said wearily:

"We would never have time to build a barrier big enough to stop them, and even if we could there are only two of us with revolvers against four sten guns, and they would be warned the moment they saw that the road was blocked."

He was right, and Larren knew it, but still he could not stand by and watch while three brave men were carried beyond all farther hope of rescue. Determinedly he scanned the road where it left the defile and curved around the base of the hill before turning off across the plain.

It was then that he spotted a new factor that neither of them had noticed before: an old man herding a score or so of cows along the dusty road below.

His body stiffened as the seed of an idea was planted in his mind. An ordinary ambush in the narrow pass would be suicide with only two men, but if the armoured car was to be stopped by a natural barrier like a herd of cows then it was possible that they could take the four guards by surprise.

It was risky of course, for if the guards were alert, trigger-happy types then he and Johnny Ling could be cut down the instant they showed their hand. But it was a calculated risk, for even though the guards might be alert for any escape attempt by the prisoners, they were unlikely to be expecting any attempt at a rescue.

Larren realised abruptly that unless he made up his mind fast he would again be too late. The armoured car was leaving Chushan and starting up the climb to the gap in the hills, and if an ambush were to be pulled off it would have to be prepared before the car passed through that gap and came in view of the plain.

Swiftly Larren rolled away from the edge of the hill and grabbed up his pack. There was no time to explain now to Johnny Ling and instead he rapped:

"Follow me, Johnny. We haven't failed them yet."

Even as he spoke he was bounding forwards down the right flank of the hill towards the plain, covering the ground in great, leaping strides.

Johnny Ling gaped and then sprang to his feet. For a second he hesitated and then he blindly followed Larren down the slope.

CHAPTER 17: AMBUSH

The old herdsman stopped and looked round slowly as he heard the sounds of Larren and Johnny Ling charging down the hillside towards him. His charges meandered aimlessly on without him as he stood and stared up at the two men who were by now halfway down the slope. His face was deeply lined and weathered and there was a wisp of white beard at his chin, and his expression was one of bewilderment rather than alarm. He carried a gnarled staff that was as twisted and knotted as he was himself, but he held it upright by his side and showed no signs of attempting to use it.

Larren reached the foot of the hill and cleared a narrow irrigation ditch that separated him from the roadway with one stride. He dropped his pack lightly on the soft earth and in the same moment drew his automatic from his belt. He had simply meant to smash the old man unconscious with the butt and topple him into the ditch out of the way, but there was something in the old man's bearing that stayed his hand. Instead of reversing the automatic he levelled it with the barrel aiming at the old man's middle and snapped:

"Just do as you're told, friend, and you won't get hurt."

The herdsman didn't understand his words but his meaning was clear enough, and they faced each other in silence in the few seconds that it took for Johnny Ling to reach Larren's side. Larren said quickly: "Tie him up, Johnny, and then put him in the ditch out of sight."

The old man spoke suddenly in a quavering tone that was weak from age as well as fear. The Chinese dialect meant nothing to Larren but Johnny answered the old man in his own tongue. The herdsman became silent as Johnny swiftly began to tie his hands behind his back.

Larren said, "You'll have to gag him too, Johnny. We can't take any risk of him shouting for help when that car comes into sight." He thrust the automatic back into his belt as he spoke, for it was obvious that the weapon was not needed. The old man was too frail to make any effort at resistance, and all three of them knew it.

Johnny tightened the last knot around the spindly wrists and then swiftly but gently laid the old man on the ground. He produced another cord from his jacket pocket and began to secure the old man's feet. As he worked he said:

"What do you plan to do now?"

Larren found a handkerchief and began gagging the old man's mouth as he answered briskly:

"I'm going to hide amongst those cows while you take his staff and herd them along the road. Keep them spread out so that the car has to stop, and then drive them right up to it. Act as stupid as you can without overdoing it and try and entice the co-driver out of the car. I'll attempt to get near enough to deal with the driver. When I do, you tackle his mate. If we can silence them without the other two in the back of the car realising what has happened then we'll be able to take them by surprise too."

Johnny's white smile flickered widely. "A few moments ago I thought you had gone mad, but now I will revise my opinion."

Larren looked at the young man and replied curtly, "It will have to be done silently. If the two guards inside the car realise that anything is amiss they'll cut us to pieces with those stens."

"It will be done silently."

Johnny still smiled but there was finality in his tone. Larren's unsmiling mouth remained hard for a few moments and then he too allowed himself a smile, and both men knew that they could each rely upon the other.

Without any further words they lifted the unprotesting herdsman and carried him between them to the ditch that ran beside the road. The ditch was shallow, a mere two or three feet deep, but it was deep enough to conceal the herdsman's thin frame. There was no more than half an inch of water along the muddy bottom and they deposited the old man gently out of sight. The pack that held their radio transmitter still lay in full view and they quickly hid that in the ditch also. Then Johnny Ling picked up the herdsman's staff and they both sprinted down the road to catch up with the straying cows.

Larren cleared the ditch again in another running jump and circled around the small herd of cattle to get head of them. The animals were lean-flanked and dirty with caked mud, and their large brown eyes regarded him almost threateningly as he stopped their progress while Johnny drove the stragglers forward. Larren threw hasty glances over his shoulder to the gap in the hills where the armoured car could appear at any moment, and swore angrily at the shying cows as they shuffled about the road.

At last the small herd was massed the way the two men wanted it, the cows strung out across the full width of the road but still bunched closely together. Larren stopped shouting and waving his arms and allowed the herd to move around him as Johnny thwacked the rumps of the rear animals and drove them forward. The large, suspicious eyes of the cows fixed nervously upon Larren as they mooed and shied away from him, they were disturbed by his presence and he could only hope that they would hide him effectively as he crouched among them.

For a few moments there was nothing to be heard except the lowing voices of the protesting cattle and the light smacks of Johnny's staff as he kept them in order, and then above those sounds came the noise of the approaching car. Larren peered above the bony haunches of the cows, wrinkling his nose against the powerful stench that they exuded, and saw the ugly steel shape of the armoured car nosing out of the pass ahead and turning towards them on the downhill curve of the road.

The cattle were still unsettled and Larren crouched as low as possible as the sound of the car's engine grew louder. Behind him Johnny Ling was shouting in a shrill, sing-song voice as he danced about keeping the cows in order, and the thwacks of his stick grew sharper and louder. The cows were hustled forward and Larren felt slightly safer as they were forced to close up around him. He took great care not to make any sudden moves that would startle them again as he moved with them.

He risked another glance over the swaying rumps and shoulders of the slowly-moving herd and saw that the armoured car had reached the foot of the hill and was now coming straight at them. Clouds of dust billowed up from its wheels as it came squarely towards them down the centre of the road.

Larren's hand moved to his hip where his beloved knife hung in its sheath, but he didn't draw the blade free. Silence was necessary, but at the same time it would be better if the guards were left alive; they were not at war and the Chinese already had plenty of grounds for making formal protests, and the murder of Chinese soldiers would not make things any easier when the British Government had to finally face the charges. Somewhat reluctantly Larren released the sheath knife and drew his automatic instead.

The armoured car was almost upon them before it screeched to a stop amid a cloud of choking dust and the harsh scream of brakes. The frightened cattle voiced their alarm with loud bellows and turned violently away. Johnny Ling still yelled frantically as he raced from side to side to prevent the herd from splitting up. Simon Larren dropped low on his stomach and peered through the jungle of shifting legs and stamping hooves to where the car had stopped a few yards ahead.

The man beside the driver was leaning out of the window and yelling angrily. He was obviously an officer of some kind but from his horizontal position on the road Larren could not distinguish his rank. Johnny Ling answered the man with a torrent of Chinese, waving his staff and hurrying the cattle forward. Larren had to wriggle swiftly along on his stomach to keep pace, at the same time twisting his body to avoid the clumsy hooves of his lumbering shield.

Through the cattle's legs Larren saw the officer step down from the cab of the car and although he could only see the lower half of the man's body he could easily imagine the expression that dominated the man's face as he shouted angrily for the cows to be moved. Johnny Ling was answering in the frantic, terrified tones of a man expecting to suffer dire punishment because of a situation over which he had no real control, and he played his part to perfection as he drove the milling cattle forward to split into two streams around the car.

Larren wriggled to the left, away from the officer and snaking past the car under the cover provided by the bellowing cattle and the dust cloud that was stirred up by their feet. He narrowly avoided the sharp edge of a hoof that just missed his face and then came silently to his feet with his back to the steel side of the car just behind the cab. He had to bottle back the need to choke and cough as his head came clear of the dust and stink and his hand was gripped hard about his automatic. Now it was up to Johnny Ling.

The young man continued to drive the cattle forward as he approached the officer. The man was young and arrogant and had a black leather holster buttoned at his hip, his face was furious but despite his fury there was no trace of suspicion in his manner. He made no effort to touch his holster as he cursed the apologetic Johnny Ling. Johnny was still cringing as the officer raised his hand to deliver a vicious back-handed cut across his mouth, but the blow never fell. Instead the staff in Johnny's hand whipped round and landed with a sharp crack across the man's temple. The young officer fell with no more than a choking gasp and Johnny caught him before he hit the dusty road.

The driver of the armoured car stiffened as he saw his officer fall, but before he could act his cab door was yanked open and a savage hand clamped around his mouth. He was dragged bodily out of the cab and then the butt of Larren's automatic descended with both force and precision on to the side of his skull and he became instantly limp.

There was a narrow grille behind the seats in the cab of the armoured car that enabled the men in the back to look out over the driver's shoulder, and although the grille was fortunately closed Larren and Johnny lost no time in dragging the two unconscious men back beneath the car where they would be out of sight of anyone who looked through.

Without hesitation Johnny donned the young officer's jacket and cap and moved around the back of the car. There was another grille set in the double doors and from behind it a pair of wary eyes peered out. Johnny had not dared to waste time in stripping the officer of his full uniform but he deftly manoeuvred one of the bewildered cows between himself and the car as he yelled at the remaining guards inside to come and help him shift the cows from the road.

Larren stood with his back to the steel side of the car and prayed that the rear doors would open, while Johnny turned his face away and began yelling above the bellows of the cattle. The cows were shifting fast and in a few moments they would be past the car and Johnny would be revealed as an impostor in a pair of baggy blue trousers, and Larren almost cried in fury as the last two guards showed no signs of coming out. Then abruptly he heard the rattle of a chain as the doors were unlocked from the inside.

The double steel doors were pushed wide open and the first of the two guards jumped down into the road, and in the same moment the beast that Johnny Ling was using as a cover took fright and bolted. The soldier gaped stupidly for a moment as he realised that it was not his officer who had ordered him out of the car, and then abruptly he levelled the sten gun he carried into firing position, at the same time yelling a warning to his companion still in the car.

Johnny Ling sprang forward in the same moment and kicked the sten clean out of the man's hands before he could pull the trigger. His fist crashed into the soldier's stomach and in the same moment he drew his own automatic from his belt.

Larren came springing round the door of the car as Johnny clubbed his automatic at the soldier's head. The man dropped away and they both looked up into the enraged face of the last guard who stood splay-legged in the back of the car. The guard raised his sten but the nearest of the three prisoners behind him lurched to his feet and threw himself bodily forwards, and both guard and prisoner came crashing out of the back of the car.

The sten gun went off in a chattering burst that chewed more pot holes in the rough surface of the road, and the herd of terrified cows finally took flight and stampeded away. The struggling guard tried to get to his feet but Larren locked one arm about his throat and delivered another savage blow from the butt of his automatic. The guard sagged and the sten clattered out of his hand, and when Larren released him he flopped down limply on to his face.

There was a momentary lull as Larren and Johnny Ling regained their breath and regarded the scene around them. Larren still held his automatic and as he thrust it back into his belt he finally gave way to the need to cough over the dust he had swallowed while worming his way amongst the cows. When he had finished the man who had hurled himself at the last guard, and who now sprawled painfully at their feet, said weakly:

"Thanks for the help, friends, but who the hell are you?"

Larren looked down into the straight gaze of the man's blue eyes and grinned. "We're just a couple of tattered pimpernels from Naval Intelligence. Lieutenant-Commander Kendall sent us out to bring you home." He added brief introductions.

The blue-eyed man winced as he tried to sit up.

"My name's Mason, Paul Mason." He jangled the handcuffs that were locked about his wrists and ankles. "The keys to these should be in your friend's new jacket," he said.

Johnny Ling swiftly searched through the pockets of the jacket he had taken from the young officer and found a large bunch of keys. He went to work willingly and within a few seconds released Mason from the two sets of handcuffs. Larren helped the Marine Captain to his feet as Johnny climbed into the car to reach the other two prisoners. There were brief exclamations as the two men were freed and then they clambered out of the car. Johnny Ling followed them, his face strangely hard.

Mason's companions were totally different types. The first man out was a young giant with an ox-like build and a six-day beard that already showed heroic proportions, while the second man was a slim Chinese man who faintly resembled Johnny Ling.

Mason said, "That's Sergeant Hugh Logan, and Chao Lin. I'm afraid we lost Tom Randell and Fen Liu when we were captured."

Larren knew now the reason behind Johnny's expression, and he glanced at his companion's face. He wasn't quite sure what to say in the presence of these men who were still strangers.

Johnny saved him from saying anything.

He said, "I think I knew as soon as I heard that one of them was dead that it would be Fen Liu. My friend also faced death if he was captured."

For a moment all eyes rested on the young Chinese man who still knelt in the back of the car. Then to break the silence Larren asked.

"How did it happen?"

Mason answered, "It happened yesterday morning. We were hiding up for the day in a large cave we had discovered when suddenly we looked out and found the whole area swarming with soldiers. There was nothing we could do but lie there until they found us. Our blasted radio had packed up so we couldn't even try to contact base." His bronzed face, which like Logan's was half-bearded, hardened as he continued. "God knows how they knew that we were there, but they knew all right. A bunch of them suddenly appeared on the hillside above us and caught us completely by surprise, not that it would have made much difference to the final outcome. Randell saw them first and jumped up in alarm, and the swine shot him down instantly. The rest of us sat tight except for Fen Liu; he tried to run and stopped a dozen bullets." He glanced at Johnny and added, "I didn't know why he ran until now — he never told us that he was wanted by the Chinese."

Hugh Logan took up the tale. He said, "We were taken down into Chushan and lodged in a stinking cell in the military barracks overnight. Then this morning we were told that we were being taken to a larger town in the north where we would be properly interrogated. This armoured car arrived a few hours later and we were bundled into it, complete with our equipment which they wanted their experts to look over. The last thing that we expected was to be rescued — I suppose it was the last thing that they expected too."

Larren grinned. "I'll explain our side of it later, but right now we've got to get the hell out of here. There's a submarine waiting out to sea to pick us up, but first we've got to get back to the coast and start swimming."

"Wait a minute!"

It was Mason who spoke, and there was a note of command in his voice. Paul Mason no longer resembled the elegant waster who had first strolled into Maclean's office to receive this mission; instead he was unshaven and ragged, and his face was a grim, bronze mask of determination.

He said flatly, "Don't think that I'm ungrateful, Larren, but we still have a job to do. As Logan said, the Chinese were good enough to load our gear in with us for the trip north, and as we still have our equipment, and now a car to take us on our way, I don't see any good reason why we shouldn't complete our mission before making our escape."

His blue eyes glinted and his voice became steely. "I've lost two good men, and I've come a damned long way just to plant a few charges of high explosive around *Vigilant*'s guts — and I'm not turning back when we're a mere sixteen or seventeen miles away."

Larren regarded him calmly for a moment and then glanced towards Johnny Ling.

"Well, Johnny? Shall we give them a hand to sabotage *Vigilant* before we make a run for it?"

The young Chinese man was not smiling now. He said harshly:

"I should hate to think that Fen Liu died for nothing."

Larren swung back to Mason. "Okay, Captain, we'll finish the job. Give me a hand to handcuff your ex-guards and we'll take them with us. It's too risky to leave them here. Chao and Johnny can put on a couple of their uniforms and drive while the rest of us travel in the back of the car."

Mason's unshaven face broke into a smile and he turned to face Logan and Chao Lin. "You heard the man — let's move!"

Within a very few minutes the two Chinese men were garbed in the uniforms of two of the soldiers. The old herdsman was retrieved from the ditch and bundled into the back of the car with the four guards. Larren gathered up his pack with the radio transmitter and followed Mason and Logan as they squeezed in beside the prisoners. He slammed the doors shut and then moved forward to draw back the shutters over the grille that looked into the front of the car. Chao Lin was ready at the wheel and Johnny Ling was now resplendent beside him in complete officer's uniform. Larren nodded and Chao started the engine. A few seconds later they were increasing speed and heading out across the plain.

With the sensation of speed a new thought became uppermost in Larren's brain. He was realising that by delaying their escape to accomplish Mason's mission he was also giving himself more time to meet up again with Reutall and Dressler. The thought brought a strange light to his brooding, grey-green eyes, a light that denoted an unmistakable desire to kill.

CHAPTER 18: DISASTER

Johnny Ling knew the country well, and under his guidance the armoured car soon left the road and turned up a rough track leading through the chain of hills that he and Larren had crossed the night before. The track was deeply rutted and in places it bulged with half-buried boulders and the car bounced and jolted violently as it wound steeply upwards. As the plain dropped below and behind them Larren briefly related the chain of events leading up to the recent rescue. Logan listened in stolid silence, but at the mention of Maclean's murder and the butchering of his family, Mason uttered a sharp, bitter oath.

After that they drove in silence until they stopped to dump their unwanted prisoners among some stunted bushes, for they were well clear of the road now, and later they would have no time to keep a constant watch on the five men.

Chao Lin drove on, fighting the wheel as best he could and attempting to avoid the deepest ruts and largest boulders, but there were times when those inside cursed aloud as the car lurched spitefully. The track grew even more rugged as the car penetrated deeper into the hills towards the sea, and it was clear that it had never been intended for any kind of motor traffic.

The sea, when at last it came into sight, appeared as a white-flecked waste of dull yellow-grey — yellow from the silt that the great rivers of China had washed down throughout the ages — and gradually faded to a darker grey where it met the horizon. The track turned south and followed the coastline.

Another fifty minutes of uncomfortable travelling passed before Johnny Ling suddenly exclaimed:

"Look! Over there — out to sea!"

Larren peered through the grille and over Johnny's shoulder, his gaze following the length of the man's pointing arm.

Far ahead he saw the sleek, proud outline of a Chinese destroyer lying motionless on the sea below; a deadly grey killer ship, her armament glinting brightly in the afternoon sun.

Mason was at his shoulder and he too saw the destroyer.

"That's our target," he said softly. "That must be the ship that was left to stand guard over *Vigilant* — and *Vigilant* will be somewhere underneath her."

Larren said, "She's still three or four miles ahead. We'd better hide the car when we get a bit nearer and cover the last lap on foot."

Chao, who had overheard, said calmly, "I understand."

The armoured car jolted on as Larren turned to Mason and asked curiously, "How would you have found your position if the Chinese hadn't marked it out for you?"

Mason grinned. "It would have been no problem; there's a small sextant in one of our packs, so I could have placed my own position from the sun and from there worked out exactly how far away I would be from *Vigilant*'s position."

"Even so, I should imagine that it will be difficult to locate the submarine once you're under water."

"*Vigilant* was a big ship, Larren, over three hundred feet long and thirty feet across, and although it won't be easy it should be possible to find her and place the charges before our air runs out."

"I hope you're right," Larren commented. "I should hate to see all the blood and action of the last week go to waste."

A really vicious lurch as the car crashed over an unavoidable boulder cut short the rest of their conversation, forcing them to cling on to their seats as they struggled to retain their balance. Johnny Ling looked back through the narrow grille and offered them a grinning apology that was too cheerful to be sincere. Then he added:

"I think it will be best if we start looking for somewhere to hide the car, before the men aboard the destroyer are able to hear the sound of our engine."

Larren agreed, and when the rising terrain around them flattened out a few minutes later Chao Lin swung the wheel and turned the car off the track. The vehicle jolted wildly over the grassy, rock-strewn ground but they kept going until the track was hidden from view by the backbone of a hilly ridge. Here Chao Lin stopped the car in a deep hollow and switched off the engine.

With an exclamation of relief Larren pushed open the rear doors of the car and preceded Mason and Logan as all three jumped to the ground. They stretched their cramped limbs and massaged a few minor bruises as Chao and Johnny came back to join them.

Larren pulled out his brandy flask and handed it round to each man before facing Mason.

"What now, Captain? Will you have to wait for dark before you can go into action?"

Mason grimaced. "I doubt if we'll have time. Those characters we left on the track back there will probably have released themselves by now, and we can't count on many hours before the hunt is up again. We'll have to try it in daylight."

"Just you and Logan?"

"No, Chao was to be reserve man if one of the sabotage party had to drop out, he'll take Randell's place. He hasn't had our training but he's an expert underwater man nonetheless."

"All right, Johnny and I will help you to carry your equipment down to the sea."

The need for speed was top priority now and they wasted no more time before dragging the three aqualungs and the two heavy packs out of the back of the car. Swiftly and efficiently Mason and Logan checked everything over. The faulty radio they jettisoned and replaced with the new set that Larren had brought, then they were ready to go. Johnny Ling again moved ahead to guide them.

They returned to the rutted track that they had followed in the car and hurried across towards the sea. As they descended the arrogant shape of the distant destroyer again came into sight from behind the hump of a hill.

Johnny said authoritatively, "We'll head straight down to the beach. From there we can keep hidden among the rocks as we move farther down the coastline."

Both Mason and Larren accepted his tone without comment; at this stage Johnny Ling was in sole command.

The climb became dangerously steep as they progressed and they were forced to move slowly and with infinite care. The patches of grass grew swiftly smaller and finally gave way to smooth, slippery rock. The heavy weight of their packs threatened to overbalance them backwards if they were not wary and at this stage they dared not hurry. Larren cursed the delay as he picked his path behind Johnny, feeling the straps of his pack cutting into his shoulders and the cold shape of the automatic in his waistband digging into his stomach as he was forced to lean forward.

Occasionally the destroyer would slide into view between the ridges of grey rock that surrounded them, but for most of the way Johnny managed to pick a path that kept them well hidden. There was no sound as they descended except the low panting of their breath and the slight scratching of their boots against the rock. They moved in single file, each man concentrating on his own personal battle to maintain both the pace and his balance.

At last they reached the foot of the hills, only a hundred yards away from the grey waves that swirled up the sandy beach. Johnny paused for a few seconds to allow the others to close up behind him and then he turned to follow the coast towards the idle destroyer. Jumbled slabs of shining black rock, some of them wet and slimy with weeds, covered the whole length of the beach below the hills, and they provided an effective screen as the five men picked their way through them.

It cost them another hour of heavy going to reach a spot directly opposite the anchored destroyer that lay approximately two to three miles out to sea; the spot that Naval Intelligence had grimly christened Disaster Point. Here they crouched among the black waste of rocks and thankfully lowered their packs.

They rested for a while to regain their breath but Mason had no patience for any further delays, and the rise and fall of his chest had barely returned to normal before he began making the final check of the swimming gear and the explosive charges. Larren eyed the six foot-long canisters of dull metal that Mason intended to sow around *Vigilant*'s vitals and said dubiously,

"They look too small to do enough damage to make the trip worthwhile."

Mason grinned. "Don't you believe it, Larren, there's enough power in these half a dozen eggs to melt *Vigilant*'s controls into a congealed mass of molten metal; something resembling a heap of half-chewed toffee was the way Maclean described it.

Three of them would do the job effectively, but we'll make doubly sure by planting all six."

Larren indicated the stationary destroyer.

"What will happen to her?"

"Nothing serious, she'll probably dance about a bit on a miniature tidal wave, and the crew will get shaken up, but there's 240 feet of water to cushion her from the actual blast."

As he spoke Mason was stripping off his outer clothing and Larren helped him into the black rubber underwater suit that he had produced from one of the packs. Logan and Chao Lin also began to prepare for their mission to destroy the secrets of the sunken submarine. All three dressed in the rubber suits and Larren and Johnny Ling helped them to adjust the aqualungs with the twin sets of oxygen cylinders across their shoulders. The last straps were tightened in place and they checked the sharp knives and waterproof torches at their waists.

Lastly each man took two of the deadly twelve-inch canisters and hooked them to their belts. Mason carried the smaller, additional charge that was to blow the conning tower hatch and enable them to enter the submarine.

Larren said quietly. "Good luck, Mason. Johnny and I will wait here for you."

Mason's voice was equally quiet. "We'll be two or three hours, Larren. We'll get as close to the destroyer as we dare before we dive and conserve as much of our oxygen as possible." He paused and then finished, "If anything delays us, you and Johnny will have to escape on your own. Don't get caught on our account."

There was a second of silence, and then a brief, faintly ludicrous moment of formality as the five men shook hands all round. Then Mason turned and led his two saboteurs towards the sea. They had to keep low among the black slabs of rock, following them where they spilled down like the scattered bricks of a petulant child to the sea. They were three clumsy shapes in gleaming black rubber, crouching and sinister, like grotesque creatures from a distant, watery world. They stopped where the grey waves burst with a low snarling into shreds of white foam among the rocks, and here they knelt to strap wide rubber flippers on to their feet. They adjusted their face-plates with equal care, and then, like ungainly seals slithering into their element, they slipped one by one into the swirls of white foam. With powerful strokes they kicked away from the turbulent water around the rocks and began to swim towards the destroyer out in the bay. Only their heads protruded above the surface as they drew away from the beach, three minute black specks in a waste of heaving grey.

Johnny Ling watched them go and then turned to face Larren.

"Do you think they can do it?" he asked doubtfully.

Larren shrugged. "If they can locate the submarine they'll do it all right. The only way they can fail is if it takes them so long to find her that they don't have time to place the charges. They've only got the oxygen for one try." He turned away and added, "They all knew the odds when they started, so they must be pretty confident. And as Mason says, three hundred feet is a lot of ship to miss if they are anywhere near it."

Johnny stared out towards the now almost invisible specks that were their companions and then he too turned away. He said philosophically:

"Whatever happens it is in their hands now — we have done our part."

They returned to the spot where they had left the remains of their equipment and found a small crack in the rocks in which to stow it until it was needed again. In one of the packs they found a plentiful supply of chocolate slabs and squares of glucose, and as the strike party no longer had the prospect of another five-day hike before being able to leave China they had no qualms about helping themselves. When they had satisfied their hunger pains they lay back among the concealing rocks and relaxed.

Once Larren used his binoculars to study the sleek form of the destroyer lying at her ease in the bay. He could see men moving along her decks but there was no haste in the movements and nothing to cause any forebodings. Of Mason and his companions he could see nothing, and for that he was glad; if he couldn't pick them out from the tumbling wave tops then it was unlikely that those on the destroyer could do so either. He lowered the glasses and offered them to Johnny who declined with a casual shake of his head. After that Larren replaced them in their case and relaxed again.

An hour passed; an uneventful hour during which the warming sun sank down to balance on the heights of the hills behind them, and in which the murmuring sound of the sea all but lulled them to sleep. Johnny Ling dozed with his eyes closed, while Larren, although wide awake, lay in the most comfortable position he could manage with his back propped against a rock slab, and deliberately conserved his strength for the renewal of action when Mason returned.

He was idly thinking that the sabotage team must by now be close enough to dive when without warning a shadow fell across the sand in front of him. His body tensed and in the same second he heard the scraping of a nailed boot on the rock above. He looked up and found himself staring into the face of a grinning soldier who was looking down at him from the pile of rock slabs that encircled their sandy hollow. The man wore the same uniform as the guards who had driven the armoured car and was holding an identical sten gun to the one that the guards had carried.

The solitary soldier looked huge and impressive from his elevated position with the scarlet sunset throwing his figure into grim silhouette. Larren stared into the barrel of the sten and knew that if he moved he was dead. In the same moment two more armed soldiers appeared to flank the first man. The sound of their approach caused Johnny Ling to sit up sharply and Larren snapped:

"Don't move, Johnny! Don't move!"

The three sten guns above them were tensed to fire, but Johnny Ling had the sense to freeze into immobility. The smiles of the soldiers became broader and triumph beamed from their eyes. Then a new voice, hissing and sinister, said softly:

"That's right, Johnny, don't dare move."

The armed soldiers stepped aside and a new figure stood between them; the tall, bony shape of Dressler. His eyes were lost behind the black discs of his glasses. In one hand he gripped an automatic and in the other his heavy, silver-headed cane. Behind him stood the dumpy, black-gloved Franz Reutall.

Dressler's teeth bared and he chuckled delightedly.

"Our old friend Simon Larren, this is a pleasant surprise. You were the last man I expected to find here. I credited you with more sense." He turned to Reutall. "This is surely a gift from Satan himself — do you not agree, Franz?"

"It is more." The little sadist's eyes were gleaming brightly. "It is the answer to a prayer."

Larren's unsmiling mouth remained closed, and his body was tensed like the compressed coil of a steel spring. He had wanted to meet these two again, but not with three sten guns looking on. Right now he could only pray for another chance.

A fourth Communist soldier suddenly appeared, stepping into the sandy hollow from a gap in the rocks only a few yards away. Dressler gave the man a curt order and he moved closer to Larren with his sten gun held at the ready. Larren still lay on his back and could do nothing except submit as the man relieved him of his automatic. The man moved over to Johnny Ling who was still balanced on his wrists and elbows where he had frozen in the act of starting up. The soldier collected Johnny's automatic too.

Larren finally risked speaking and demanded.

"How did you get here, Dressler?"

The thin man smiled. "Franz and I were on our way with this four-man escort to meet and accompany the prison van that was bringing your spy friends from Chushan. Unfortunately for you we found one of the guards you had to leave behind; he had managed to release himself and then ran all the way back to the main road. He collapsed from exhaustion, but not before I had learned that the fools at Chushan had been stupid enough to transfer Mason's gear in the same car. I guessed that he would try to complete his mission and wasted no time in getting here."

His thin face hardened and he snapped:

"Where are Mason and the other two?"

Larren ignored the question while Johnny Ling continued to glare. But the answer was obvious. Dressler simply stared over their heads out to sea and then rapped out a battery of orders to the four Chinese soldiers.

Instantly the three men who stood beside Dressler on top of the rocks leapt into the hollow. Two of them stood back with their stens menacing the prisoners while the other two soldiers jabbed them into movement. Dressler jumped down more cautiously as Larren and Johnny were forced to their feet, while Reutall followed by a more laborious route.

"Move, Larren," hissed Dressler sharply, although the order was completely unnecessary in view of the jabbing guns. "I can guess where Mason and his men have gone, so don't attempt to waste my time with any delaying tactics."

He snapped more commands at the Chinese soldiers and the next moment Larren and Johnny Ling were being propelled roughly along the beach. The thrusting sten guns kept prodding them savagely in the ribs and forced them forwards at a stumbling run. Larren's mouth was dry as he realised that those stens could easily burst into a spray of accidental fire from the careless way the soldiers used them, and he did his best to keep ahead.

They left the cover of the rocks and were forced away from the beach. After several minutes of violent, nerve-racking running Larren saw a crude stone building that was presumably the home of some fisherman rising out of a dip in the ground ahead. His pace faltered for a moment and there was another snarling command from Dressler and a quick dig from a gun barrel to drive him on. The four soldiers herded their two prisoners at a run towards the barn-like hovel.

As they covered the last few hundred yards Larren saw two vehicles parked beside the building. One was an army jeep and the other was a large black saloon. His mind had no time to dwell on them, however, for he and Johnny were pushed roughly past and into the building.

Inside there were just bare stone walls, a rickety cupboard of split planks and an uncovered table and a few chairs. The floor was bare earth. Dressler ordered Larren and Johnny Ling to sit at the table and place their hands on their heads, and when they had obeyed he turned to Reutall.

"Watch them, Franz, keep them covered every second. I must reach a telephone and try to get a warning passed on to the destroyer. They can send divers down to intercept Mason and his men, if it is not already too late. Larren we can deal with later."

Dressler flung the last of the words over his shoulder as he ran for the black saloon, and a few seconds later the car's engine roared into life. The four soldiers were now standing back patiently with their stens trained unerringly on Larren and Johnny Ling. Reutall watched them with his automatic in his hand.

Larren could only boil with silent, helpless fury.

CHAPTER 19: "FOR YOU, ANDREA, MY DARLING"

Larren knew that if he was to do anything to save Paul Mason and his two companions from being ambushed under water then he would have to act fast, but with sten guns and Reutall's automatic pointing directly at his head there was absolutely nothing he could do. He glanced desperately at Johnny Ling, but the young Chinese man was glowering under the threat of the two remaining stens and was equally helpless. Outside the building the black saloon was snarling noisily as Dressler backed it up and turned the bonnet to face the rough track that led north along the coastline.

Larren tensed as he heard the car accelerate and his hands parted slightly where they were clasped above his head. The movement was seen and instantly the nearest soldier thrust his sten close against his face, the ugly steel barrel was no more than three inches from Larren's eyes.

Reutall said softly, "Sit still, Larren. Sit very, very still."

Larren had no choice. He sat in the crude wooden chair beside Johnny Ling with his hands on his head and murder in his eyes and heart. He could do nothing but listen as Dressler revved the engine of the black saloon and drove away.

The sound began to fade and Larren glared without speaking into the hated, cherubic face of Franz Reutall. The little sadist beamed back at him, the gleaming, black leather gloves that covered the scarred brand marks of the letters S.S. giving to his appearance an evil touch that more than outweighed the shortness of his stature. Johnny Ling scowled at the armed soldiers and then turned his gaze through the open door to the sluggish, yellow-grey surface of the sea that was still visible below them.

There was no way of knowing what was passing through Johnny's mind as he stared down the beach, but Reutall suddenly glanced at him with a look of deepening suspicion on his face.

"What are you looking for?" he demanded. "What are you thinking?"

Johnny turned his head to answer the little man's stare, but his mouth remained shut.

However, Reutall did not wait for an answer. Instead he smirked suddenly and said, "I know what it is! You are hoping that your friends will return in time to help you. You hope that they will realise that something is wrong when they find that you are not waiting for them." He was enjoying his role and his voice purred on. "Perhaps your friends will return much sooner than Dressler and I expected — but that will not help them, or you. For I shall be waiting for them in your place."

Still smirking Reutall rapped brisk commands to the four soldiers and then turned his gleaming eyes back to Larren. "The two men who will remain with you have orders to shoot if you make the slightest move," he said silkily. "But please don't force such an act upon them, for I would prefer you to be alive when I return. And do not worry about your friends; if Dressler's warning does not reach the ship in time, I will catch them as they surface."

With a final, curt command to his men Reutall turned and hurried out of the building. Two of the Communist soldiers followed at his heels as he led them down to the beach, while the two remaining men moved threateningly closer to the prisoners.

Larren watched Reutall until he was out of sight, the loathing for the black-gloved killer gnawing like a cancer into his heart. For the moment the black rage that swirled in his brain prevented him from thinking clearly, but slowly he realised that Reutall's misinterpretation of Johnny Ling's gaze had cut their guards by half, and that now the odds were even.

He looked back into the wary eyes of the two guards and bitterly revised that last thought; the two sten guns made the odds far from even, and a man could die just as quickly from two streams of bullets as he could from four.

Larren's mind was still a crazy turmoil of half-formed, hopeless plans as he sought for an avenue of escape, when suddenly Johnny Ling broke the strained silence. He still had his hands clasped obediently above his head and his voice had a nervous, faltering note as he spoke to the nearest soldier in Chinese. Larren only understood one word, and that was the word for cigarette.

The soldier snarled an unmistakable command for silence.

Johnny insisted in a meeker, whining tone.

The soldier bellowed another angry command and pushed his sten gun hard against the young Chinese man's temple. Larren stiffened and the second soldier glared at him and raised his own sten. Johnny Ling was cowering back in his chair, his hands still tight upon his head, his whole body seemed to be trembling but still he mumbled another pitiful plea for a cigarette.

Larren could only watch with the taste of fear rising dryly into his throat. He couldn't guess what Johnny was trying to do, but there were two facts that he was sure of: one was that the young Chinese faced almost certain death once he was recognised, and two was that he did not smoke.

Larren wanted to cry a warning to his friend; a desperate plea not to take any suicidal risks; but he could only remain watching, his muscles tensed to follow the young man's lead.

Johnny Ling continued to cringe and beg for his cigarette and the uniformed soldier practically screamed him into silence. The man was glaring angrily and a final, almost inaudible whimper goaded him into violent action. He jerked the barrel of the sten away from Johnny's temple and raised the weapon for a vicious blow that would drive the butt hard into Johnny's teeth.

It was the moment that Johnny had been working for, and in the fraction of a second that the gun was reversed and the barrel no longer pressed against his temple he acted. His cowering body uncoiled from his chair with the muscular lighting of a striking snake. His head butted the soldier savagely in the lower abdomen and the man uttered a gasping shriek of agony as he doubled up under the impact. Johnny was already underneath the sten gun and the soldier dropped the now useless weapon and tried clumsily to grapple with him with his hands. The man's mouth was still gaping open as Johnny's fist came up to smash into the point of his jaw, the blow slammed his teeth together with a sickening smack and sent him reeling away.

The soldier who had been covering Larren swung round as Johnny Ling moved. The brief scuffle as Ling felled his man was over in a matter of seconds and before Johnny could turn the second soldier opened up with a burst of shattering fire. A stream of bullets ripped across the width of Johnny's shoulders from close range, hammering into his broad back and almost slicing him in half. The sound was deafening in the small room and the impact smashed Johnny towards the far wall, transforming his back and shoulders into a mess of shredded scarlet.

Simon Larren was unable to stop the guard from cutting down his companion, but before the man could swing the sten gun back to cover him again he too had acted. He came out of his chair with a speed that almost matched that of Johnny Ling and dived for the guard's throat. They crashed down together and Larren employed every dirty trick in the book to render the man insensible; he clamped one clawing, throttling hand about the windpipe and used the other to gouge murderously at the staring eyes. At the same time he smashed his knee repeatedly and with hideous force into the most vulnerable part of the man's body. It was doubtful whether any man alive could have survived the concentrated fury of that attack, and within a matter of seconds Larren had clubbed the guard unconscious with a final, terrible blow of his fist.

He was on his feet and spinning round to face the second guard before his own victim had fully ceased his struggling, and for a fraction of a second they faced each other through the faint haze of death and cordite that still lingered from the burst of gunfire. Then the still-gasping soldier dived forward in a frantic lunge towards his fallen sten.

The soldier was barely halfway there when Larren literally threw himself across the room, his flying body smashed into the guard and sent him spinning back to the ground. Larren himself had no choice but to finish by crashing face down on to the bare earth, but even as he landed he was rolling unhesitatingly towards the fallen sten. His fingers closed around the steel barrel and he came up on to his knees, aiming the sten in a vicious swing at the sprawling soldier in the same sweeping movement. The butt of the sten gun connected with the base of the man's neck as he tried to struggle up and he slumped back to the ground for the third and final time.

Larren changed his grip on the sten into a firing position, and for one fleeting instant of time he stayed on his knees to survey the scene around him. Both guards lay completely senseless and the twisted, bloodied form of Johnny Ling lay crumpled in the violence of death against the wall. Larren stared at his friend, knowing that Johnny had committed deliberate suicide in order to give him this slim chance of life and freedom. Then he realised that Reutall and the remaining two soldiers must have heard the sound of firing and be even now racing back, and he must not let Johnny's sacrifice be in vain.

He sprang grimly to his feet and crossed to the doorway of the house, and as he looked down towards the beach he saw the two guards racing back with Reutall lagging behind them. The two soldiers saw him as he stepped into the doorway and both of them halted simultaneously, but even as they steadied their weapons Larren's finger was tightening round the trigger of his own sten. The gun snarled hideously and spat a murderous stream of lead towards the two men. Larren aimed low and deliberately cut their legs from under them.

As the two soldiers screamed and fell away Franz Reutall came to an abrupt sliding stop, his lips peeled back from his tightly-clenched teeth in a frightful expression of hate and rage. He thrust his arm up and forwards and his black-gloved hand tightened convulsively about his revolver.

Larren dropped down on to one knee as Reutall fired and two shots whined through the doorway above his head to smack into the far wall behind him. The revolver had kicked back in Reutall's grasp and before he could level it again Larren had brought his sten to his shoulder. The fact that he was technically a spy on neutral soil had prevented Larren so far from killing outright any Chinese soldiers, but there was nothing between heaven and hell that could stop him from cutting down this vile and hated creature who had helped to arrange the murder of his wife so long ago. His face became a granite mask and his grey-green eyes burned with the lust to kill, and seven softly chilling words escaped from his unsmiling lips.

"This is for you, Andrea, my darling."

And then he squeezed the trigger of the sten.

The shuddering, chattering burst of fire picked up Reutall like a dry leaf caught in a gale; it tore through the dumpy body and smashed the revolver from the black-gloved hand, drowning the first single shriek of agony that was the only cry that the little sadist could utter. For a brief second the twisted form was suspended in the air, jerking like a ping-pong ball in a fairground shooting range; and then at last the sound of the sten gun ceased and the corpse lay still.

Larren rose slowly to his feet and walked closer to the remains of Franz Reutall, he felt that there was something right and just in the way that Reutall had died, for his beloved Andrea had also been cut down with a sten gun. A warm feeling of inner satisfaction stole lethargically through his frame, and then suddenly he remembered Dressler.

Reutall had been just a pawn in Dressler's hands, for it was Dressler who always gave the orders; and Dressler was hurrying to warn the Communist Headquarters with almost ten minutes start.

Instantly the ice flooded back through Larren's veins and he turned and ran towards the jeep that had transported the four soldiers. He swung his body behind the wheel and dropped his sten gun on to the seat beside him as he started the engine.

The jeep roared into life and simultaneously Larren slammed it into gear. He wrenched hard at the wheel to bring the vehicle slewing round to face the track that Dressler had taken, and then stamped the accelerator down to the floorboards. The jeep practically flew down the track.

Larren braced his body as the jeep crashed and swayed crazily beneath him, concentrating his whole being on driving the vehicle to its full limit. He wanted Dressler, and that was all that mattered now; Dressler, the last of his wife's murderers. The danger to Mason and his men was not forgotten, but it was his long-dead wife and his own dark vendetta that dominated his mind.

Deep below the surface of the sea Paul Mason was beginning to despair in his task of finding the sunken *Vigilant*. The powerful beam of his torch cut through the dark watery gloom; picking out the beckoning tendrils of the flowering underwater ferns that pushed up from the muddy floor of the seabed; picking out rising crags of deeply-pitted, shell-encrusted rock; picking out the swiftly-darting shapes of fish of all sizes and a hundred different silvery hues; but never picking out anything that could remotely resemble a sunken submarine. On either side of him he could see the patches of torchlight that marked the progress of Hugh Logan and Chao Lin, the bodies of the two men were invisible in the blackness behind the torches and the two splashes of light moved eerily through the undersea world.

They were swimming at a critical depth, below which it would be impossible to operate, and already the severe pressure was causing Mason's head to throb and his heart to race at almost treble speed inside his chest. He knew that it was quite possible to black out under this fearful, crushing strain, and he wondered how much longer they would be able to hold out. Already they had used half their air supply and if they did not locate *Vigilant* soon then it would be of no use to locate her at all.

Despite his doubts he swam on, probing the inky depths with his torch, propelling himself swiftly and easily with strong thrusts of his legs. The three charges that hung from his waist had been clumsy at first but now he hardly knew that they were there. Now he was only aware of the pressure, and of the need to find *Vigilant* fast.

More waving ferns and crusty ridges of coral rock passed below him, a great shell gaped at him from the seabed, and a school of tiny fish suddenly appeared in front of him and then were gone, like a swiftly-driving cloud of silver rain. Then abruptly the splash of light that moved fifty feet to his left began to flicker on and off in an excited signal.

Chao Lin had found *Vigilant*.

A sense of triumph swept through Mason's frame, and for the moment the deadening effects of the fierce pressure were forgotten. He flashed his own torch towards the second circle of light that moved on his right-hand side, and a few moments later the huge, cumbersome shape of Hugh Logan glided through the gloom towards him. Mason waited for the Sergeant to catch up and then together they swam to join Chao Lin.

The Chinese guide hovered with slow movements of his flippers, his body upright and his eyes gleaming behind his face-plate. As they neared him he extended his arm and pointed with his torch into the silent blackness of the sea. Mason and Logan joined him and saw a vague outline like the smooth front of a massive, double-decker bus rising out of the seabed just within the limits of their vision. All three swam slowly towards it and in the combined light of their torches it slowly took shape as the blunt bows of a submarine.

They paused to read the name *Vigilant* above them, and then Mason led the way as they swam alongside the submarine's hull. *Vigilant* had settled on the muddy bottom with only a slightly-angled list to port, and she lay in majestic silence as if only an order was needed to send her disdainfully on her way. They passed below the tall, dominating conning tower and then stopped as they saw the cruel rent that had torn open her hull. Mason drifted closer, no longer doubting that it was an internal explosion that had sent the gallant ship to the bottom. He moved carefully along the length of the gash and saw that the tangled metal inside and jagged edges of the hull itself would make it too dangerous for them to enter that way. He turned to shake his head significantly so that his companions could understand and then swam upwards.

Logan and Chao Lin followed him up on to the smooth, flat surface of the submarine's deck. The tall conning tower rose into the darkness above them and the water swirled around their fins as they continued upwards. They reached the bridge of the sunken vessel and Mason pulled himself down to the hatch cover. He had no time to waste and he swiftly clamped the smallest of his charges into place. The charge was of the magnetic type and adhered to its position with a dull clang. It was timed to explode within three minutes of making contact and swiftly Mason rejoined Chao and Logan and led them away.

They swam back along *Vigilant*'s deck and took shelter below her bows as they waited. The weird vastness of their surroundings tensed their muscles even more than the expectation of the explosion, and *Vigilant* loomed dark and sombre above them The murderous pressure made itself felt again and Mason was aware of a new throbbing behind his eyes. All three of them stirred their fins slightly to keep themselves from floating away from their shield.

Then the gentle crunch of the explosion sounded dully through the depths of their underwater world, and the vibrations sent faint ripples through the sea.

They began to swim back to inspect their handiwork.

The explosion that had smashed in *Vigilant*'s conning tower hatch cover had been too small and too deep to be picked up by any human ears on the surface. But the Chinese destroyer that lay above for the express purpose of making sure that no new submarine sneaked in to destroy the one already there possessed instruments far more sensitive than human ears. The slight disturbance beneath the sea was noted and reported to the ship's Captain, and a swift battery of orders started a chain of activity throughout the ship.

Within a very few minutes a team of four Chinese divers was preparing to slip over the side and investigate. Each man checked the razor-sharp knife at his hip before descending beneath the surface.

Simon Larren drove his stolen jeep with the demented skill of a suicide pilot who could desire nothing more than a violent but glorious death. The untidily-looping coastal track that he followed would have made fifteen miles an hour an uncomfortable speed, but Larren drove the jeep flat out. The vehicle shrieked and protested as it bounded insanely from one jolt in the track to another, and the tyres shredded and burnt as they skidded across the stone-littered earth.

Larren himself felt as though he was being torn apart by a dozen straining stallions all being whipped into a frenzy in a dozen different directions. It seemed that at any moment his arms must be dragged from their sockets or his whole body pitched from the cab, but somehow he held his seat and fought the twisting wheel. He knew that no man and no car could possibly survive this for long, but still he kept going, and his only prayer was that he should be allowed to catch up with Dressler before the jeep spun out of control down one of the steep slopes to the sea.

He knew that he must be gaining rapidly, for despite his start Dressler would barely be doing half this speed, but still Larren maintained his reckless pace. Disaster Point was many miles behind him now, and it seemed that this spitefully-writhing track must follow the coastline for ever. From time to time he received brief glimpses of the darkening sea, for a dusky twilight was taking the place of the setting sun, but eventually the track began to swing more inland and there was nothing on either side but the craggy ridges of the barren hills.

Almost half an hour had passed since Larren had settled the score with Franz Reutall, and the punishment he was inflicting upon the jeep was nothing compared to the battering that the jeep was inflicting upon him. But no amount of battering could dull the burning spur of vengeance that goaded him on to the final clash with the last of his wife's killers. As he had murmured in the brief moment before Reutall died, this was for Andrea; not for Mason or Kendall, or even the dead Maclean and his butchered household, but solely for Andrea.

The shadows were lengthening now, and the world was blurred by the half darkness that lingers between the setting of the sun and final nightfall. The poor light made an additional driving hazard, but Larren was determined to refrain from using his headlights for as long as possible. Dressler would be able to spot the lights in his mirror long before he could hear the sound of the jeep's engine, and Larren meant to give him as little warning as possible.

He had to strain his eyes to follow the direction of the track ahead and more ruts and boulders made the jeep bounce erratically beneath him. A few more crashes like that and he knew that the jeep's axle must inevitably snap, but still he refused to relax his foot from the accelerator. Then quite suddenly a beam of light sprang into life through the hills ahead and below him, and elation gripped him as he realised that the beam could only be the headlights of Dressler's car. The man was still half a mile ahead of him but the gap was closing rapidly.

Larren concentrated everything into his driving during those last few suicidal miles, and gradually he drew ever nearer to the large black saloon. Dressler was driving with more regard for his car and was keeping his speed down to the realms of sanity, and within a few minutes Larren had his enemy clearly in sight. Inexorably the gap narrowed until at last Larren could see the outline of Dressler's head and shoulders through the rear window of the saloon.

Larren was still driving blindly without lights and he cut the distance between the two vehicles to fifty yards before some sixth sense warned Dressler that he was being pursued. Larren saw the outline of the man's head twist round as he looked over his shoulder and then the black car began to leap ahead. Instantly Larren flicked on his lights, and the bright arc of the twin beams settled like the relentless probe of a searchlight on the car in front.

Dressler was pushing his foot hard down, but the black car needed a few minutes to pick up to the speed of Larren's jeep, and in those few minutes the jeep gained another ten to twenty yards. Larren smiled savagely as he watched the gap lessen and then reached calmly for the sten gun that had long ago been thrown on to the floor near his feet. He transferred the sten to his right hand and gripped the steering wheel with his left. His thumb released the safety catch as he leaned his body half out of the jeep and he pulled the short sten gun firmly into his right shoulder. The black saloon car was brilliantly illuminated in his headlights as he aimed the sten at the vehicle's rear wheels. Then he fired a long, chattering burst.

Strips of shredded rubber flew from Dressler's exploding left rear tyre, and the back end of the black car swung round in a great slithering half circle. Completely out of control the car bounced off the track and plunged down the steeply sloping hillside to the left. There was a great, shuddering crash as the car heeled over and a high-pitched scream from the man inside. The car bounced helplessly on its side and then a second reverberating crash pitched it completely over in a final death roll. There was the last teeth-grating tear of tortured metal and then at the last the car came to a standstill at the bottom of the slope. Miraculously it had rolled back until it was standing the right way up.

Larren had been forced to drop the sten as it had kicked back viciously when he fired, and he had to grab desperately at the wheel of his jeep to prevent it from following Dressler's course down the hillside. Now he fought tensely to control the jeep and then braked it to a skidding halt fifty yards farther down the track. The jeep stopped with a final jolt and Larren sprang down and raced back to where Dressler's car had disappeared.

He reached the spot just as the petrol tank exploded and the black car burst into sheets of flame below him. He stopped to stare, and in that moment he beheld the most incredible and horrifying sight that he had ever witnessed.

The door of the black saloon was thrust open and Dressler struggled out; Dressler with his clothes and hair blazing and his mouth open in one continuous scream of agony; Dressler who stared up at him as he stood gazing down the hillside, and then came charging up the slope towards him: Dressler who was now reduced to a blazing ball of agonised flesh, motivated solely by a still-living spur of hatred.

CHAPTER 20: MOMENT OF VENGEANCE

Even Simon Larren had to flinch from the terrible picture that Dressler presented as he rushed up the steep slope of that hillside. The man was bathed in flame and clawed at the earth with his hands and feet as he moved almost on his hands and knees. His horn-rimmed glasses were somewhere in the fiery wreckage behind him and his weak eyes were bulging at bursting point from his head. He had lost both his revolver and his silver-headed cane and he came forwards with his bare hands alone. His crazed screams rang with hideous echoes above the snarl and crackle of his blazing car.

Larren had no weapon left now except the sheath knife that still hung at his hip and he barely had time to draw the blade free before the final moment of vengeance and horror was upon him. He had to fall back from the sheer, insane fury of Dressler's attack, the flames from the man's burning clothes seared his face and the gruesome smell of burnt flesh sickened in his nostrils as the groping hands sought for his throat. He crashed down to the ground beneath the weight of the impact and terror chilled his soul as the man's shrieks of agony pierced his eardrums.

He could feel the flames transferring themselves to his own clothes as he struck home desperately with his knife. He buried the blade to the hilt in Dressler's body but it seemed that nothing could stop the fiery, pain-strengthened hands that clutched at his throat. Dressler had passed the ultimate peak of pain by now and it had left him as nothing more than a maddened monster that fed upon hatred and revenge.

Larren writhed frantically beneath the mass of living flame that was choking away the last shreds of his consciousness, and somehow he dragged his sheath knife free. He struck again and again and with each blow the creature above him screamed and shuddered.

Larren was on the point of blacking out when at last the fiendish grip about his throat began to slacken slightly. He made a last superhuman effort to tear the throttling hands away, and even as he did so he realised that Dressler had stopped screaming. He struggled from underneath the still-burning body and realised slowly that Dressler was dead. Not even the man's madness could sustain him after those deep, killing thrusts of the knife.

Larren crawled away and rolled his body weakly over in the wet grass that flanked the track in order to put out the flames that had begun to smoulder on his own clothes. Then he collapsed and lay face down on the earth while Dressler's corpse still smoked and the black car blazed furiously to the night.

By the time Larren had recovered enough strength to stir the car had burnt itself to a skeleton and a cold night wind was moaning softly through the hills. Larren rose unsteadily to his feet and found that the stained sheath knife was still gripped fast in his hand. He replaced the weapon at his hip and then moved with faltering steps towards Dressler. The man made a ghastly corpse and he soon turned away and staggered back to his jeep.

Dressler was dead, and the dark vendetta was over, and now he could concentrate on the fate of Paul Mason and his sabotage party. He had to get back to Disaster Point.

The explosive charge that Mason had planted on the hatch cover of the sunken *Vigilant* had done its work well. The heavy steel hatch had buckled and was half open, and with the powerful muscles of Hugh Logan to help him Mason soon had the hatch right back. He shone his torch down into the conning tower and for a moment there was a respectful hesitancy in his manner, for it was impossible to forget that the sea was a grave and that *Vigilant*'s steel hull was a giant coffin for over a hundred brave men.

Then slowly Mason pulled himself down head first into the hatch, disappearing like some great black fish into its haunt. The silence and the pressure were almost unbearable as he pulled himself down the ladder into the submarine, and his lungs and heart seemed as though they all wanted to burst open together inside his chest. He twisted his body and shone his torch back through the hatch, lighting up the crouching shape of Hugh Logan; the Sergeant's eyes were weirdly distended behind his mask, and the fine black beard that fitted his face so well above water now sprouted strangely around his lips where his teeth were closed around the mouthpiece of his aqualung; the round curves of his two oxygen bottles protruded above his shoulders like sinister humps. Mason signalled to him to follow him into the submarine.

Logan swam down without hesitation and Chao Lin was left alone to remain on watch while the others did their work. It had been arranged on the beach that the Chinese guide was merely to take the dead Randell's charges down to the submarine and then stand guard while the two experts placed them in position. Now he could only watch as the twin beams of torchlight sank deeper into the interior of the sunken *Vigilant* and finally vanished altogether in the watery darkness.

There was something distinctly eerie about being left alone on *Vigilant*'s bridge, and Chao felt a chill that was not due to the temperature of the water circulating through his bloodstream. He stared down at the long deck, his gaze following it as far as he could see in the range of his torch and then straining his eyes into the inky depths beyond. A strange, cold sense of power swept through him and it was as though the gods of the sea had given him command of this silent, shark-like ghost of the deep. He had to shake his fancies away and he knew that he would be glad when the job was over. *Vigilant* was a tomb and would be best left undisturbed.

The minutes crawled by, each one clinging defiantly to every distended second of its allotted time. Chao glanced repeatedly at the waterproof watch on his wrist and tried to will the two men inside the submarine into more speed. Their time was getting short and soon they would have to start back for the surface for they could not ascend swiftly without succumbing to the terrible cramp that came from the sudden changes in water pressure. But unless Mason and Logan hurried they would have to run that risk, or else never reach the surface at all.

However, the sowing of those deadly seeds of destruction that the two Englishmen carried was a job that could not be hurried, and Chao Lin was forced to wait while they were placed with infinite care against the most vital parts of *Vigilant*'s secret equipment. Three of the evil canisters were distributed with their hollow clanging sounds about *Vigilant*'s control room and attack centre, each one carefully placed in accordance to the instructions that had been issued by the experts back in Hong Kong.

Both Mason and Logan had to steel themselves against the sight of the bloated bodies of the crew that stared with sightless eyes from all sides, and Mason's stomach began to revolt as he worked. When he had placed the last charge in the control room he led the way through the underwater corridors towards the launching room for the armament of Polaris missiles that *Vigilant* carried. Here they placed their last three charges with equal care.

The dull, slightly reverberating sound of the last magnetic charge clamping itself into place sent a surge of relief through Mason's frame. The job was done, and now they could get out. He and Logan were invaders here; invaders committing foul sacrilege in an underwater grave. The open eyes in some of the dead faces they had passed seemed to stare with shocked disbelief, and the water they had disturbed had caused some of the swollen bodies to sway menacingly towards them. There was resentment here in this dead ship, resentment and pain that emanated from the lost souls to whom she was both a monument and sepulchre. They had no right to come here to destroy; no right to mangle any farther the men who were already dead.

For a brief moment he looked into the face of his companion and saw that behind his mask Hugh Logan was similarly disturbed. It made Mason feel a little better to know that he was not alone with his thoughts and emotions and he jerked his head grimly to indicate that they should leave. Logan nodded his head in solid agreement and one behind the other they swam back through the dead silence that was as oppressive as the fearsome weight of the sea. Their only thought now was to get away from this dark world of fish and ghosts; away from the ugly, ticking canisters that were timed to release their shattering destructive power within ninety minutes of being placed into position; and away from the taste of death and slime and back to the clean-smelling freshness of air that could only be breathed above the sea.

On *Vigilant*'s bridge the agony of waiting was playing havoc with Chao Lin's nerves. The torch in his hand moved consistently as he played the beam along the dim outline of the submarine, or tried to pick out the fern and coral formations on the seabed below. However, he found it impossible to distract his mind from Mason and Logan and every few seconds he would direct the beam down into the conning tower in the hope of seeing them return. Each time he was disappointed and gradually the fear that some accident must have befallen them became almost a certainty in his mind. The thought nagged at him and he became prey to indecision as he wondered whether or not he should defy his orders and dive down to find them. It was while he struggled with this problem that he suddenly became aware of four separate splashes of light descending through the darkness above him.

Fear gripped Chao Lin, cold fear that was pumped through his body with every beat of his speeding heart. But he did not panic. For a moment he stared up at the four pale, slow-moving torch beams and then he quickly switched off his own light. Total and absolute darkness fell upon him, the deep, cold darkness of the bottom of the sea.

Chao resisted the near overpowering urge to light up his surroundings again and groped around the conning tower for the open hatch. His fingers found it and he hesitated for a moment to glance again towards the approaching lights. Four lights could only mean four men; four enemy frogmen. The thought made the fear circulate more thickly through Chao's veins but he ignored it and pulled himself down into the invisible tomb of the submarine.

His hands found the steel ladder that led down from the hatch and he pulled himself rung by rung as he entered, and then suddenly there was a glimmer of light below him. Chao had never felt so great a need to offer a prayer of gratitude in all his life, and he was almost sick with relief as Mason and Logan swam up from the control room below.

Mason gave a start as he saw the black, rubber-clad form suspended head downwards in the light of his torch, and then the head twisted round and he recognised the staring eyes of Chao Lin behind the mask. Chao pushed himself away from the ladder and his body writhed grotesquely as he straightened himself up.

Mason could only look at him in bewilderment as he wondered what the hell was happening. Then Chao gestured to the now extinguished torch at his belt and then pointed upwards through the hatch, then he held up four fingers, and finally he drew the knife from his belt and held it in readiness.

Mason and Logan both understood, they drew their own knives and switched off their torches, waiting in the pitch blackness.

There was no sound and they might each have been suspended alone in an inky vacuum as they steeled themselves to meet the coming clash. Mason's dark thoughts returned in a chilling torrent and he wondered whether this was some ironic decree of justice on the part of some leviathan god of the sea; to be trapped and killed here in the very grave they had despoiled. The vile pressure of the sea held them fast and they could only wait and fear.

The next few minutes were the worst that any of them had ever faced, the strain on their nerves was crippling and the tension built up into a great, smothering, invisible force around them. Then slowly the blackness above them became less complete and a glimmer of light reflected down through the hatchway. The light grew stronger and they realised that one at least of their enemies was swimming down on to *Vigilant*'s bridge.

They heard the slight clang of the diver's boots on the steel deck, and the sudden break in the silence tightened the tension almost to snapping point. The full beam of the diver's torch was now concentrated on the ruptured hatch cover above them, and Mason knew that at any second they would have to surge out and fight. To retreat and attempt to play hide and seek in the bowels of the sunken submarine would be fatal, for already their air was running low and they had no time to waste if they were to escape the terrible, choking death of drowning. Then suddenly the light above became a blinding white ball that radiated its powerful glare straight into their eyes as the enemy diver directed his torch down the hatchway.

The stabbing beam struck the crouching form of Chao Lin and instantly the Chinese guide surged upwards with violent thrusts of his fins. He attacked blindly, his eyes screwed shut against the brilliant white light and his knife sweeping up against the pressure of the water to stab at the man outside. His rush carried him clean through the hatchway to tangle clumsily with the enemy. The man had his own knife in his free hand and they threshed and twisted together in the sea, their bodies lifting up and away from *Vigilant*'s bridge with the momentum of Chao's charge.

Three more shadowy shapes closed in on the struggling pair, moving like swift grey tiger sharks with the scent of blood in their gills. Chao felt the body in his grasp stiffen and arch backwards as his knife struck home, and in the same instant he felt the cutting bite of steel in his own flesh. The three remaining Chinese frogmen swirled around him, their torch beams clinging like stage spotlights to his desperately twisting form. The man he had killed sank away and in the same moment Chao saw the slow flash of a second knife coming towards him and felt again the bite of a keen blade.

In the same moment Mason and Logan emerged from the sunken *Vigilant* and surged together into the attack. The disturbance of the water caused the three Chinese frogmen to wheel and face them, and then the five men closed together in a silent duel deep below the sea. The torches were dropped as they grappled clumsily with knives, but as they were all attached to the belts of the wearers they did not sink and instead jerked and dangled crazily to light up parts of the scene. The crushing pressure made it impossible for the fight to be settled quickly and they squirmed and slashed with little effect in the watery weightlessness of their silent world.

Like weird sea monsters that had only just learned how to crawl out of the slime of the seabed they battled backwards and forwards across the submerged deck of the motionless submarine. Three against two, circling and weaving warily through the depths, no man wanted to close in case an enemy should sink a knife into his back while he fought, but Mason and Logan both knew that they did not have the time that was on the side of the Chinese.

Mason chose to attack and surged again towards the nearest frogman, he flattened his body as he thrust with his fins and at the last moment twisted through the depths to avoid the other's knife. He rolled clear of the thrust and came up to curl one arm about the man's throat. The remaining frogmen darted together towards Mason's exposed back but the huge, dangerous shape of Hugh Logan swam between them.

The two frogmen hesitated and then separated as if by some secret signal. They circled the Sergeant and then rushed him simultaneously from both sides. Instantly Logan wheeled and thrust himself towards the nearest of the two. They met head-on in a violent tangle and Logan clamped one hand around the other's descending knife wrist. As he did so he arched his shoulders away to escape the attack from behind. He heard the clang of steel hitting against the oxygen bottles that protected his back and then the movement of the sea had carried both himself and the man he held out of range.

Mason still clung tenaciously to his chosen victim and struggled to draw his knife arm back for a blow. He had his legs locked around the diver's hips and he was hanging on to the man's back despite the intervening air bottles, but the man was holding equally tightly to his knife wrist and was preventing him from striking to kill. The water swirled and bubbled around them as they tumbled through the depths and then abruptly Mason managed to wrench his arm free. He raised his knife and struck once, plunging the blade deep between his opponent's ribs.

He allowed the body to sink away and turned to search for Logan and the other two frogmen, and in the jerking lights that hung from their belts he saw two divers grappling together and the third circling behind them. He swam swiftly towards the scene of battle, but even though his own torch was still switched off and he approached in darkness the third man sensed him coming and wheeled away. Mason hesitated for a moment and then realised that the two wrestling together were locked in a trial of strength; each man was holding off the raised knife of the other with a firm wrist grip as they fell slowly towards the seabed. In the crazy, dancing light Mason was not sure which was Logan and which was his enemy, but one thing that he was sure of was that the husky young Scot possessed all the strength he needed for a contest of that sort.

Grimly Mason left the violently-writhing pair behind him and swam in pursuit of the last of the four enemy frogmen.

He could see the bobbing light of the torch that trailed from the man's belt moving through the sea ahead, and swam strongly after it in the pitch darkness. The fleeing diver was either too frightened or too low in intelligence to switch off the guiding light and simply vanish into the watery darkness, and Mason gradually closed with his quarry.

His head was aching furiously now and he knew that he had already stayed too long at this critical depth, and had been subjected to far too much of this frightful pressure, but he also knew that that last Chinese diver had to die. If the man lived to report back to the destroyer then the sabotage party would be captured as soon as they surfaced.

With this thought spurring him on Mason concentrated the last of his strength in a burst of driving speed that brought him within range of that trailing beam of light. The torch showed up clearly its owners threshing legs and fins, but the rest of the man's body was lost in the darkness beyond. Mason's eyes were fixed on those furiously-kicking legs as he squinted behind his face-mask. Then he lunged one hand through the swirling sea and gripped his quarry's left ankle.

The diver twisted in terror, his body distorting itself wildly as he fought to get free. His efforts were futile for Mason slashed once with his knife and sliced the blade through the tendons behind the man's knee. The crippled diver twisted in silent, helpless agony as Mason released him, and he could do nothing as the Marine Captain surged in again for the final kill.

Mason hovered in the blackness as he watched the last body sink to the bottom, and then slowly he sheathed his knife and fumbled for his torch. He switched the torch on and began to swim slowly back to the sunken *Vigilant*.

After a few minutes the blunt bows of the submarine again rose above him from the seabed, and a few seconds later he saw two clumsy figures in aqualungs still entwined together. For a moment he thought that Logan must still be caught up in his duel to the death, but then he realised that the two men were not fighting but that one was helping the other. Logan had won his trial of strength and now he was towing the seemingly lifeless Chao Lin.

Mason failed to recognise any signs of life in Chao's limp form, but he reasoned that the Sergeant would hardly be wasting time with a corpse and so did not hesitate to help. Together they swam away and upwards, carrying Chao Lin between them.

They had to ascend gradually to avoid too swift a change in the sea pressure and swam at a gentle angle that would bring them to the surface well away from the destroyer overhead. They were hardly aware of the eerie darkness of their undersea realm now, for both of them were suffering badly from the gruelling strain to which they had been subjected ever since they had first dived below the waves.

Their fast-decreasing supply of air was another source of worry and Mason repeatedly glanced at the tiny gauge that was incorporated in the aqualung outfit. It was clear that they were going to break the surface with very little to spare, and he tried not to think of what would happen if they could not reach the surface at all.

The merciless pressure slowly eased around them and at last they were swimming comfortably on the last stretch of the climb. The water was still as pitch black as it had been on the seabed below and Mason realised that it must now be night up above. When he judged that he was within twenty feet of the wave tops he switched off his torch, for its light could betray them to the men aboard the destroyer if it remained on, and they had to make the last part of the ascent again in darkness.

There was never a sweeter moment than the second in which their heads finally broke through into the night air. Both men tore off their masks and spat out the mouthpieces of their breathing tubes. They sucked in eager mouthfuls of the cold, invigorating air, and the effect freshened them immediately. The dark silhouette of the destroyer was over half a mile away from them, and they still had two miles to swim to the shore, but after what they had just been through not even ten miles could have soured this moment.

They supported themselves with gentle movements of their fins as they regained their breath, and after a few moments Mason remembered Chao Lin. He pulled off the guide's face-mask and found that the man was still alive although unconscious. There was nothing that they could do for him until they got him back to the beach so they grimly began their swim, still towing the man between them.

The broad fins on their feet gave them an advantage that an ordinary swimmer would have lacked, and despite their burden they were able to make good progress without any exceptional effort. Both in the sea and under it they were two of the strongest swimmers in the Royal Marines, and even after an ordeal such as the one they had just been through they were still in their element. The fresh, salty air cleared their heads as they maintained a steady, rhythmic pace and the shoreline grew swiftly nearer.

In just under an hour they were in sight of the beach and could hear the crashing of the waves among the black rocks. As they covered the last hundred yards they saw the dark shadow of a man rise up from a mass of boulders, and they were unable to suppress the frightening thought that they had swam straight into another trap before they heard the softly calling voice of Simon Larren.

Mason called out in answer and Larren came down to the beach to meet them as they kicked through the last few yards of breaking waves. Larren saw the way that Chao Lin slumped between the other two and quickly plunged into waist-deep water to assist them up the beach. Between the three of them they carried Chao clear of the spraying wave crests and laid him gently in a patch of soft yellow sand.

Larren said grimly, "What happened?"

Mason and Logan stared at him, and then Mason said:

"We could ask the same of you?"

Larren glanced down at himself and even in the darkness he realised that he made an awe-inspiring sight. His clothes were scorched and blackened and great stains of Dressler's blood covered the sleeve of his jacket. He also knew from the way his face smarted and burned that his eyebrows and part of his hair had been singed away.

He said: "It's a long story, Captain, but it's over now. The worst part is that Johnny Ling is dead."

Mason swore bitterly. "Not Johnny too! How the hell—"

A sudden, menacing rumble echoed in from the sea, swelling up from the depths where the sunken *Vigilant* lay. The sound cut through Mason's words as they all turned to stare, and they saw the dark outline of the distant destroyer rear up like some disturbed monster on the dark horizon. The ship lurched drunkenly from the terrible expanding pressure that rushed up from below her and her bows seemed to dip momentarily beneath the waves as her stern leapt clear of the water. She settled back none-the-worse from her shaking but the rumbling sound continued; it rolled across the bay in the form of a miniature tidal wave some three feet high, gathering speed with a growling roar as it rushed towards the beach.

The wave smashed into the black rocks, surging through them and knocking the three men sprawling to the sand. The spray flew high and the snarling rush reached its limit and began to swirl back to the sea, sucking and drawing at the sand and rocks and dragging at the three struggling men and the limp Chao Lin. Larren closed one desperate hand over Chao's wrist and held him until the last swirl had retreated and died.

Silence stilled the night and then Mason said quietly:

"That's it, gentlemen. Mission accomplished — and *Vigilant* destroyed. All we have to do now is to get back to base."

CHAPTER 21: THE LONG SWIM

Without any further waste of time Mason and Logan swiftly unharnessed their aqualungs and stripped off their black rubber suits. Mason found to his surprise that he had collected a shallow knife gash along his forearm, but although the wound began to smart savagely the moment it was discovered it caused him no serious inconvenience. The two Marines dried themselves and dressed hurriedly, and then they turned to help Larren to attend to Chao Lin.

Larren had already removed the man's aqualung and suit and they found that Chao had received two nasty knife wounds; one had gashed open his left side below the ribs and the second had pierced his thigh. However, nothing had penetrated his vital organs and although he was still unconscious it was clear that he would soon recover with proper care. They bandaged and dressed him as well as they were able and then Mason said:

"We'd better get going, we've got a long way to carry him before we get back to the armoured car."

"No need," Larren said. "I've got a jeep waiting above the beach. We can use that."

More questions faltered on the tip of Mason's tongue, but he held them back until some more suitable time. Instead he helped Logan to carry their aqualungs and unwanted gear out on to the rocks that thrust into the sea and hurl them into the waves out of sight. The only things they retained were the swimming fins they would need to swim out to *Watchful*.

Larren retrieved their radio from its hiding place among the rocks and then they carried the helpless Chao Lin up the beach towards the jeep. Even when they passed the shattered corpse of Franz Reutall and the four injured or unconscious soldiers, whom Larren had tied up safely on his return, Mason and Logan still bottled up their impatience to know what had happened. Not until they were speeding south in the jeep with Larren at the wheel did they finally give way and ask him to explain.

Larren obliged, and by the time he had finished the track they followed had passed the spot where they had left the armoured car. Larren drove carefully, for the jeep had already taken a terrible hammering when he had pursued Dressler in the opposite direction, and the last thing he wanted was for the axle to break now. They reached the point where the track branched off through the chain of hills to the broad plain and ultimately Chushan, but here a narrower track continued to follow the coastline and it was on to this track that Larren turned the jeep.

They drove in silence now, each man alert and half afraid that they would find the hills alive with swarms of Chinese soldiers, for the alarm over their escape must have been raised several hours ago. However, the black, silent hills were empty, and if the hunt was on then it had not yet reached this part of the coastline.

Larren's keen gaze searched the night beyond the range of his headlights, and eventually he saw a sandy bay down to his left where the track swung closer to the sea. It was not the bay where he had landed with Johnny Ling, but it was near enough to do. He reasoned that they must be a good fifteen to twenty miles below Disaster Point, which was far enough south for

Watchful to surface without being seen by the destroyer, and that was all that mattered.

He drove the jeep down on to the sand and stopped while Mason and Logan jumped down and unloaded Chao Lin and the few remaining items of their gear. Then Larren drove the jeep straight for the sea. He pushed his foot hard on the accelerator and the tyres skidded hellishly and sprayed up clouds of the soft sand. The speedometer reached twenty-five before the jeep ploughed into the breaking waves and Larren kept his foot down as the water smashed over the bonnet. The sea flooded into the cab and only then did he push himself clear. The roaring of the jeep choked and drowned in the battering waves, and Larren waded up the beach as the vehicle came to rest with half a foot of water breaking over her roof.

Hugh Logan had already doubled back to smooth out the wheel marks where they had left the track, and after five or six minutes work on the rutted sand there was nothing to show that the jeep had ever crossed this lonely beach.

Once their trail was covered they retreated up the beach to another protective screen of boulders, and here the two Marines calmly took an hour's rest while Larren kept an alert watch. The sixty minutes crawled by in dawdling silence, broken only by the soft swirl of the surf and the hooting cry of a nightbird somewhere in the black mass of the rising hills. Slow clouds obscured the moon but faint starlight relieved the darkness, and Larren could see clearly the relaxing shapes of his companions. At last, exactly on the hour, Mason sat up and professed himself fit to go.

Logan stretched and raised his bulk to a sitting position, but Larren eyed them both dubiously.

"Are you sure? You've both done a lot of swimming already tonight."

Mason smiled. "I've done twelve-mile swims before, and so has Logan. Of course, we don't usually try it after a long jaunt on the sea bottom, but I reckon we can manage it." He glanced at Logan. "Isn't that right, Sergeant?"

The bearded Scot nodded. "We can do it, but —" he looked at Larren — "can you?"

Larren grinned. "You don't necessarily have to be a Marine to know how to swim. But what about Chao?"

Mason answered, "Logan and I will take him. You'll have to take the radio and the flash gun for signalling. You'll have Chao's fins, and with those to help us we should make good progress."

There was no more to be said, the matter was settled and a few minutes later they were wading out into the sea. They had paused only to use the radio to contact *Watchful* and check that she was still out there waiting for them, and now there was nothing left to do but face the long, weary swim.

Twelve miles is not really a great distance when compared to the efforts of those who swim the width of the English Channel merely for the sake of breaking records, but despite the confidence of the two Marines it was still a marathon that was to exhaust them all. The broad rubber fins strapped to their feet gave them an invaluable advantage, and without them it was doubtful whether they could have ever reached the safety of *Watchful*. But the still-unconscious body of Chao Lin proved a dragging burden, and even the light radio transmitter on Larren's shoulders began to weigh heavily as the hours and the miles passed in slow company.

Throughout the night they laboured on, settling into a steady, unchanging rhythm of movement. Larren resisted the urge to turn his head and look back, for the retreating shoreline never seemed to get any farther away, and instead he concentrated in keeping in time with the calculated driving strokes of Mason and Logan. Salt waves broke in his face and started new fires against the patches of singed flesh, but even that discomfort failed to prevent him from feeling the cruel cold of the sea as it soaked him to the marrow. Above there was the faint glimmer of the stars, and all around them the heaving, watery blackness that stretched ahead to infinity.

The strain wore at them all, tearing at muscles and tendons, sapping their strength and crumbling the will to go on. Their pace grew slower as they succumbed to the rigours of cold and exhaustion, and their movements became more laboured and their breathing more painful as they swam on. Nothing existed any more except the sea, the terrible weariness, and the defiant need to stir their feeble limbs forward as they fought to stay on the surface.

Larren suffered worst of all, for he lacked the stern training that aided the other two despite their burden, and he was both mentally and physically exhausted when the first grey streaks of dawn began to relieve the darkness, fading the pale stars slowly out of existence. He was hardly aware of what was happening as Mason left Logan to support Chao and swam towards him. He felt Mason fumble with the waterproof transmitter that was strapped to his back and tried to remain steady as the Marine Captain ran up the short aerial. They bobbed clumsily on the waves as Mason called up the waiting submarine.

Watchful had been lying at periscope depth with her radio antenna raised above the surface to pick up the call when it came, and almost instantly the submarine rose above the sea like some smooth grey monster less than a quarter of a mile away. The sight inspired Larren to find the last shred of strength needed to draw the flare pistol from his belt and shake it free of its waterproof covering. He pointed it upwards and fired once. A spray of bright red stars burst in the dawn sky above them and immediately the sleek outline of *Watchful* surged forward to pick them up.

Captain Allendale commanded his ship with the skill and precision of an expert, and eight minutes later the swimmers had been neatly fished out of the water and the klaxons were blaring the order to dive, dive, dive, throughout the submarine. Two stalwart ratings carried Chao Lin to the sickbay while others helped Mason, Larren and Logan into the officer's wardroom where dry blankets and steaming mugs of rum-laced tea awaited them. Above them the sea swirled to a close over *Watchful*'s hull as she slipped back into the dark, shielding depths.

The scalding brew in the brimming mugs began to slowly thaw the chill from their bones as they sat huddled in their blankets, and they sat in silence as the driving screws took them swiftly away from the distant land mass of China. They were on the last stage of the journey home, but this moment was reserved in memory of the men they had left behind; Sergeant Tom Randell, Fen Liu, and the gallant Johnny Ling.

Then slowly their thoughts turned from the past to the future, and Paul Mason began to wonder whether the blonde that he had so abruptly left on Repulse Beach would still be waiting for him.

Hugh Logan closed his eyes wearily and dozed into a mental picture of heather-clad hills and glens and the blue skies of Scotland, and with it came the memory of a lass he had always fancied but never asked.

And Simon Larren? He held a fleeting thought of Maxine Kia, but knew that it would be kinder for her if she never saw him again. And from there his mind probed deeper into the past, back to a grey and sombre day beside a small cemetery outside the city of Paris. He knew that this must be his last duty now; to return to his cherished Andrea, and to whisper softly that she had been fully avenged.

A NOTE TO THE READER

Dear Reader,

In today's publishing world online reviews are vitally important and if you have enjoyed my work please spare the time to write a review for **Goodreads** and **Amazon**, or just a complimentary mention on any media platform.

If you want to contact me you can do so through **my website**. I am always pleased to hear from readers. In the meantime I will get on with the next Falcon SAS novel for your enjoyment.

Sincerely yours, Robert Charles

Sapere Books is an exciting new publisher of brilliant fiction and popular history.

To find out more about our latest releases and our monthly bargain books visit our website:
saperebooks.com

Printed in Great Britain
by Amazon

80244324R10136